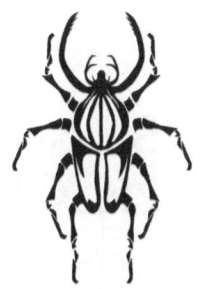

Immortal
Shadow

by Anderson Atlas

Book #3 in the Heroes of Distant Planets series

a Prequel

Synesthesiabooks.com
520-869-9649
thelostspells@gmail.com

This book is a work of fiction. Names, characters, places, and in-cidents either are products of the author's imagination or are used fictitiously. Any resemblance to actual events or locales or persons, living or dead, is entirely coincidental.

Name: Atlas, Anderson
Title: Immortal Shadow
Description: Trade paperback edition 2: Synesthesia Books, 2016
Identifiers
ISBN-10: 0-9974788-5-3
ISBN-13: 978-0-9974788-5-3
Subjects: Dictator, rebellion, Teenage hero,
BISAC: Juvenile Fiction / Fantasy & Magic
Wholesale Available from IngramSparks

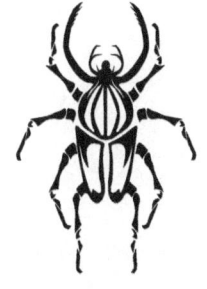

Immortal
Shadow
by Anderson Atlas

Book #3 in the Heroes of Distant Planets series

a Prequel

Anderson Atlas

Chapter 1
The Testing

Jibbawk was a lean creature even for his nine-foot stature, much leaner than the other Shadics he would compete against today. Jibbawk, like all Shadics, was covered from head to toe with poisonous quills. Some were longer than others, but they were all as sharp as hypodermic needles. Jibbawk used his long beak to pinch a quill on his forearm and run the length through his beak in a grooming fashion. He liked to be clean, so he did this often. Other Shadics weren't so thoughtful about their appearance. For instance, Maddawk, the Shadic behind him was balding because dirt clumps clogged his follicles. He also smelled as foul as the Dedite Slicks, the very swamp the empire used to decompose dead servants and criminals. There was another reason Maddawk was so foul. His fore-fathers killed Jib-ki-bawk, Jibbawk's father. It was a distant feud between the Mad and Jib families, but as fresh to Jibbawk as a bleeding slash across his back.

Jibbawk and twelve other Shadic slaves, shackled by their feet and hands, were lead through tall archways lined with pearl-white tiles and lit by enormous skylights thirty feet overhead. Jibbawk was fourth in line, but he felt like he should have been first.

The slaves stopped at a smaller hallway guarded by a Shadic female. She was much shorter and her quills were hidden by armbands, neck collars and ceremonial tape that covered her body. She used

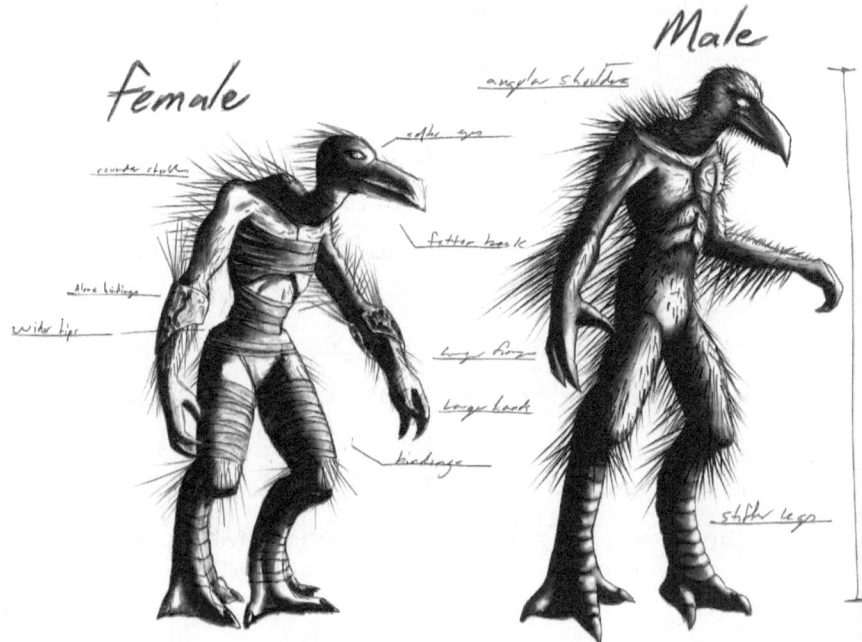

a long thick key to unlock the shackles that bound the first Shadic's wrists then led him down the dark hallway and out of sight. She said nothing, but didn't have to.

Fifteen minutes later, another Shadic was taken down the hall. Twenty minutes later another Shadic left. None returned, although they were supposed to.

Jibbawk's turn came. He walked down the narrow hall. There were no lights along the way and the closer to the end Jibbawk got, the darker it became.

Jibbawk reached the door at the end. There was no handle so he waited. Finally, it opened. Light blasted him and his red irises focused to pin points. He stepped into the light while simultaneously plucking two long quills from each forearm, holding them like daggers.

Shapes came at him like arrows. Jibbawk could barely see in the light, but it didn't matter. He could see well enough. He stabbed the flying creature, keeping the long quill in his hand.

Jibbawk took a step, but there was nothing below his feet. He fell.

He reached out blindly, grabbed a branch and

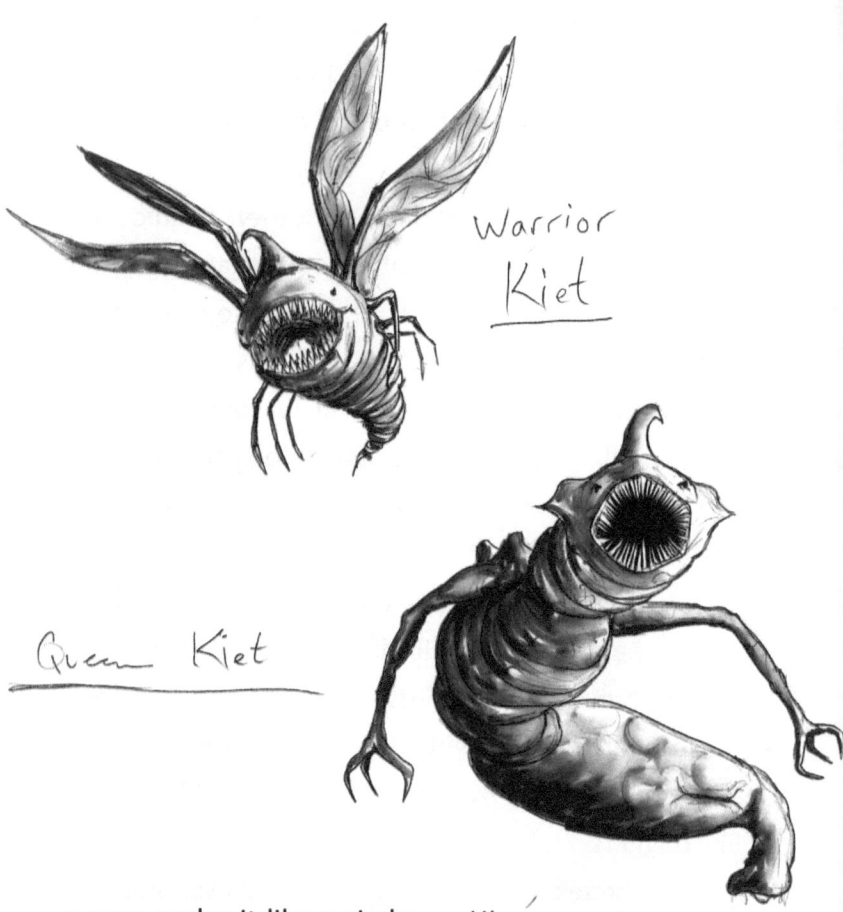

Warrior
Kiet

Green Kiet

swung under it like a circlown. His momentum spun him all the way around the branch. He kicked and released and landed on a thicker branch. He executed his move efficiently and just in time, too.

His eyes had adjusted to the bright light only to see a handful of the flying creatures barreling to-

ward him. They were kiets. Kiets had long, plump bodies, six legs, two with sharp claws, and a mouth full of razor-sharp teeth. Shadics normally hunted kiets for their delicious thorax juices, but taking on one or two was far different than a whole swarm of them. Trying to breach their nest to get eggs, was near foolishness. The closer one got to their hive, the more vicious they became. Obtaining just one egg was a suicide run.

Jibbawk threw his quill and landed it inside a kiet's biting mouth and leaped out of the way of another one. He landed on another branch and leaped again. Jibbawk's powerful, clawed feet and beak were the only feature that still resembled the birds from which Shadics had evolved.

The buzz of wings vibrated the air. Jibbawk flung out an arm, releasing shorter quills. Three kiets were impaled and fell to the forest floor, over two hundred feet below. Jibbawk jumped to a gnarled, dangling mossy plant and pulled himself up to another branch.

Up the tree he climbed, batting off and stabbing attacking kiets. When he neared the crown of the tree, he saw the Queen. She was bigger than Jibbawk had imagined. Her long body was wrapped around the trunk. She was laying eggs along the underside of the tree branches, sticking them with gelatinous slime. Surrounding her were hundreds of freshly hatched kiets and a dozen very large warriors. One dove at Jibbawk, but he leaped off the branch, catching another with his hands. The warrior kiet flew past and turned midflight. Jibbawk swung back and forth dodging others. As one flew passed Jibbawk snatched its wing, ripping it off. The kiet spun and fell, making a shrill cry.

Jibbawk plucked quills and flung them with skill and speed only years of practice could explain. Soon his forearms were bare, but he had more on his upper arms. Jibbawk was fast, almost a blur. The kiets were persistent, blind to the death and raining out of the tree like falling leaves.

Jibbawk negotiated every attack until he reached the branch on which the Queen sat. She screeched loudly at him, opening her round mouth filled with a hundred barbed teeth. She could easily survive Jibbawk's poison. Hundreds of her loyal children were returning from foraging.

Jibbawk leaped at her. She screamed, unafraid of him. She snapped, repeatedly. He snatched her thick throat with one hand and plunged his other

into her body. Blood sprayed on Jibbawk as he pulled out her heart. Once she was dead, the other kiets went into a fury. One slammed into Jibbawk and knocked him in the head, another clamped onto his back and bit off a dozen quills and another tore out a chunk of Jibbawk's leg muscle. He didn't cry out or stop. He simply reached down to where the Queen's tail pouch started and ripped it off like it was nothing but a leech cloth covering a lantern.

Inside the pouch was what Jibbawk wanted, eggs.

Jibbawk dodged another attack and took another bite on the forearm. His head was about to be severed by the snapping teeth of a warrior kiet, so Jibbawk let go. He fell like a meteor.

Half-way down he reached out and grabbed a string of moss. His fist clamped shut, stripping the mossy clumps from the stem as he fell. His descent slowed until he came to a stop. A few more leaps down and Jibbawk was on the very branch that led to the hallway he'd come from. It was a tunnel delicately carved into the side of a mountain of solid stone.

The door opened, and Maddawk came out. Jibbawk pushed past him, dragging the egg-filled end of the queen behind him. Maddawk looked at the tail and was visibly confused. He backed away from Jib-bawk.

Jibbawk passed the other Shadics who all, once seeing the queen's tail behind him, gave him a wide berth. He emerged from the long hallway to a large room that curved sharply to the right. The female key-keeper stood and gaped at the egg sac. She hurried Jibbawk around the curve and into a huge viewing room. The back wall, floor, and ceiling were covered with the same pearl tiles. Hundreds of seats twenty rows high filled with Shadics of every shape and size and status. The opposite side of the great viewing room was a very thin, razor-sharp mesh. They could see the entire tree from here.

Jibbawk strode easily past a hundred Shadics. The more powerful a Shadic was, the more quills were taped down or hidden by cloth. Jibbawk being a slave, was barren of dress, tape or adornments.

At the end of the crowd was a section for the elder Shadics, which included the Resident Ruler, Cal-Kaw and the High Priestess, Ixawk.

Cal-Kaw had a traditionally clipped beak, another sign of his superiority and his quills were wrapped by metal arm bands and a golden-laced bandage. Further hiding his body was a cloak made

from the scaled skin of minit sea serpents. At first glance the scales looked white, but a rainbow of colors reflected off them in the bright light. He smiled. "So you've brought us the queen's tail, have you?" Cal-Kaw leaned back in his great throne carved out of a reddish marble and cushioned with a sponge-like padding. "You've done well. I am pleased."

The crowd burst into applause.

"Yesssss, I'm glad you are pleased," Jibbawk said, rolling his 's'es like a serpent.

Ixawk placed her hands together reverently, her eyes beaming. "You are either very brave or very foolish of only which your survival will judge." She was required by law to pluck every last quill from her body so her lean, powerful shape could be seen by all who were allowed to look upon her.

Jibbawk laid the sac at Ixawk's feet. His blood mixed with the slime of the pouch and pooled on the stone floor. "I'm just doing my duty as bessst as I ss-see fit." Jibbawk believed his lineage to be the oldest and most powerful, but there was more to it. He knew he was to be the first of the Infinite Rulers, but didn't dare say it in front of Ixawk or Cal-Kaw.

The oldest stories say that the Shadics must conquer all the habitable worlds in the galaxy and those that succeed will become immortal and will rule forever. Ever since Jibbawk was a youngling in training, he knew he would be the first Infinite Ruler and that all others would bow before him.

"You have brought us sixteen eggs and so will be awarded one point for each. I've never given out so many points before." Ixawk looked over Jibbawk's wounds. "You may wrap yourself before the next challenge. I look forward to seeing what you'll do next," Ixawk's dark skin looked almost soft between the large pores where quills use to grow, and her eyes were as red as Jibbawk's. She stood and waved a servant over to her. "Take the eggs and prepare them for the final feast."

Ixawk took two gold armbands and cupped them onto Jibbawk's forearms. They pinned down a section of longer, more dangerous quills called the flalanx quills, which had tapered edges and flew straighter and farther when thrown. They also had the most potent poison. "I hereby issue these; alanx-bindings imbued with the seal of the great ruler. They symbolize your victory here and are proof to all that would oppose you that you do not need your flalanx quills to conquer your enemies."

Jibbawk bowed deep and for a long time be-

fore he was led away by a younger slave to be bandaged. As he passed a couple of elders wrapped in various colored cloaks and adorned with sparkling jewelry, one leaned to the other and said. "No one has ever killed the Queen. I did not think it could be done by one slave Shadic. Contestants are only required to scavenge a few eggs to pass this test."

Before Jibbawk left the great hall, he heard the resident ruler Cal-Kaw call out to the crowd. "Let Maddawk begin his test. For his sake, let there be more eggs to collect." The crowd roared.

Jibbawk was bandaged tightly and led to a waiting room. There he stayed until all the Shadics in the Trials today got to fight the kiets and collect the required amount of eggs for the feast. It was the first of three tests. It tested strength and agility and was a hallmark of the Shadic race.

The others completed their test; Maddawk collected more eggs than the rest, though he could only carry eight. Jibbawk was not surprised.

Anderson Atlas

Chapter 2
Of Time and Stillness

The Testing continued. Jibbawk followed a beckoning female slave out of the stadium's large foyer. She was wrapped from head to toe in tight black bands. The black symbolized her failure at the Testing. "So you will be a sslave for all time?" Jibbawk stopped her and looked into her unusually beautiful, orange eyes.

She bowed her head. "I'm overjoyed to serve for my life. I did not prove my value at my Testing."

Jibbawk mused at her pleasing shape. "You will accompany my government when I am victorious." His claw cut one of the bands that wrapped her long neck. "If you wish," he said, standing close.

"I would be honored."

The two continued past the towering marble pillars that framed the entrance to the coliseum-like structure that had been built out of the mountainside and into a crowd of onlookers, some booing, and some cheering. Enormous shadic guards, carrying long spears, parted the crowd and let the contestants by. Beyond the stadium steps and parked along the mossy pathway that snaked around other pearl-white buildings were a line of wood, open air carriages on skis that glided over the thick fuzzy moss that covered ninety percent of the wetlands on planet Aton. Pulling the slipdo was a marishtic, a creature with a large round body covered in claw-like protrusions that went every which way, a tiny head, and a hundred padded legs.

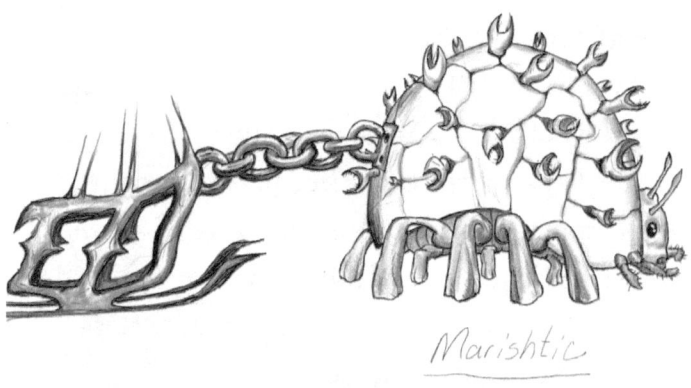

Marishtic

Jibbawk boarded the back of the slipdo and stood, holding a railing as the marishtic took off at a reckless speed. The beast of burden easily negotiated rock outcroppings, over rolling hills of thicker, pale-green moss and around the thorn bushes. In front and behind Jibbawk were dozens and dozens of

various vehicles, some with as many as ten Shadics in the carriage.

The procession traveled away from the city of Cicanth, the capital where all homes and buildings were required to be made out of the pearl-white tiles. The city was orderly, bright on the green moss and extended to the horizon.

Along the outskirts of Cicanth was a swampy wetland filled with enormous trees that towered overhead, their leaves as big as warrior shields, many with patches of dangling moss hanging from their branches.

The slipdos passed the wetlands and headed into the hills that were covered in thick teal moss. They stopped at a small valley, the center of which were large acid baths. Jibbawk and the other contestants was escorted to the top of a cliff that hung over the bubbling pools.

A huge wood contraption at the top of the cliff dangled a dozen thick ropes with short stools on platforms attached to the ends. Jibbawk and the others reached out, grabbed their seats, sat and swung out over the acid baths. The platform under the stool had perches on either side intended for the contestants' feet to grip onto to achieve balance. This was the purpose of the test, to show mastery over the smaller movements of the body.

The crowd gathered around the baths, remaining a safe distance away from the caustic, corrosive spring. The stone at the edges of the liquid was smooth, the same pearly white stone the city was made of, but the acid was muddy black and scalding hot.

The planks were held to the rope at the back and moved wildly as the Shadics found their balance.

Jibbawk closed his eyes and pressed his back into the rope, feeling the tension and micro-movements. He found stillness first with his clawed feet gripping the perches below the seat. As the others fought the tipping and swinging, Jibbawk picked his feet up and crossed them in the front. The crowd gasped. Jibbawk teetered, but remained upright.

One of the younger Shadics, seeing how the crowd loved Jibbawk's grandiose display, attempted to cross his legs but tipped wildly and was dumped. The Shadic fell into the baths with a thick splash. The acid was as viscous as sludge, but as hot as molten steel. He screamed and flailed as his body burned. Soon he sunk below the surface and was gone. It only took seconds for the acid to melt the quills, skin, muscles and organs. The bones would disintegrate within a few days.

Maddawk scowled at Jibbawk. He attempted to cross his legs but returned them to the perches. A gerot Shadic took bets on who would last the longest while the riled-up crowd watched and waited.

A slave filled a white stone bowl with the acid and walked it up to the top of the cliff. He gently poured the steaming liquid into a channel on top of the contraption. The acid ran down a dozen stone groves that led to each rope.

The crowd chanted shadic names and clapped in a rhythm intended to distract the contestants and disrupt any inner peace. The acid pooled at the rope ends and started to eat away the fibers. Over time, the rope strands would snap and eventually the platforms would plunge into the acid. The Shadics were to remain on the seat for as long as possible. Whoever lasted the longest would win the most points.

Smoke steamed from the top of the contraption like chimneys. The acid ate away a strand of Maddawk's rope and his seat fell an inch. He almost lost his balance but kept it.

A Shadic next to Jibbawk suddenly fell after his rope gave way.

The individual strands of the thick rope snapped, one at a time. Jibbawk could feel his rope weaken. Once it fell, there was no way to jump off it and reach safety. So you had to anticipate the break. He gritted his beak together. He has to outlast the others. It was his destiny.

The gerot waived his hand at the balancing shadics. "You have all achieved your league. You may save yourselves."

Some of the weaker contestants leaped to

safety. They would pass this test, but not achieve greatness. The collected points would reflect only one winner.

Every few moments a shadic leaped off the platform to safety.

Smoke from the burning rope thickened and the crowd grew louder. A Shadic tried to jump away, but failed and was pulled into the belly of the black bubbling stew. There were only four left now. One jumped off, as he felt himself get too close to the acid. Then another. Maddawk's second-to-last strand snapped, his platform only inches from the acid. He screeched in frustration and jumped, leaving only Jib-bawk.

Jibbawk had won. The light warmed his skin and the sudden burst from the crowd sent ripples of oobumps across his skin.

He uncrossed his feet but a moment before he could jump the rope snapped. Jibbawk didn't jump for the shore; that would have only sent the chair backward and him into the hands of the acid. No, he jumped up. Jibbawk had planned for this. He let the platform perch hit first then landed on the top of the stool. The extra second of time allowed him to jumped again. The crowd gasped as Jibbawk spun in the air like a twirling dorvit. He hit the edge of the bath and rolled away. A splash burned the back of his neck, but he did not react to it.

The crowd broke into the loudest roar. No Shadic had ever survived the fall of the seat.

Jibbawk was presented to the Resident Ruler, Cal-Kaw, and the High Priestess, Ixawk again.

Ixawk bowed to Jibbawk. "You continue to impress me, Jibbawk." Her vivid red eyes twinkled in the bright daylight. She took a round awk crown and placed it on Jibbawk's head, pinning down more quills. The cap was an intricately carved oxit shell inlaid with gold. "This crown is very rare and entitles you, Jibbawk, to a Sixit of land on any planet." The crowd approved. "It covers even more of your quills. As you achieve greatness, your body will eventually all be taped. This represents power, for only the lowest of our society do battle with their quills, muscles and spears. The greatest of us use our wit, our position and our intuition to best our enemies. Greatness means never having to fight your own battles."

Chapter 3
Test of Wit

Without rest or delay, the slipdos took the remaining Shadics back to the city. There was much discussion and adoration as onlookers glared at Jibbawk from their seats and covered perches. They were in the presence of a master Shadic.

The procession passed large stone buildings, smelters, guild schools of every discipline, modest homes and grand mansions. They rode over the green moss quietly, workers and other alien races, watching them pass. The slipdos arrived at the city center. Towers surrounded a large courtyard of bright green moss. Huge bonfires burned at the apex of each building without end. In the courtyard was a ring of tall trees with only one, thick trunk and three or four enormous leaves at the top. Inside the circle was a large amphitheater of white marble seats and a stage along one side rimmed in gold and surrounded by smaller fire pits.

Jibbawk got off his ride and strode into the tree circle, the seven remaining Shadics behind him. The elders, Cal-Kaw and Ixawk, gathered on the stage and sat in thrones. Ixawk waved Jibbawk and the others to a row of seats beside the rulers. Jibbawk sat quietly and waited for the others.

Cal-Kaw spoke loudly, the crowd respectfully quieting down. "This is your final test. You will arrive near an Ophex outpost. Your challenge is to overtake the outpost and return a strange talking box to us. If you survive, you will be rewarded with freedom. If not, it is because you are weak and you will not serve the Shadic Empire in any meaningful way."

Ixawk placed a clawed hand on Jibbawk's shoulder. "Every kill will gain you five points. You all know what awaits the Shadic who gains the highest count."

Jibbawk did. The winner would be given their own planet to rule. He not only wanted dominion over his own world, he expected it. He was born of royal blood and though he had served as a slave for twenty years, he still trained at the best pods.

Ixawk bowed, dipped her claws into a ceramic jar and sprinkled a pinch of Hubbu pollen over Jibbawk's head. The Hubbu flower produced an exotic

pollen that somehow opened wormholes to other, similar, planets. Hubbu flowers of different colors produced pollen that went to different worlds. Shadics had been using the various Hubbu colored flowers to travel across the galaxy and not only inhabit other worlds but to rule them.

The Hubbu pollen cascaded in a spiral pattern around Jibbawk and created sparks. The sparks connected and drew a bubble over him. When the bubble popped, it folded Jibbawk into the fabric of netherspace and spat him out on the planet Nophan.

In short order, the seven other Shadics arrived, dozens of feet apart.

They were surrounded by tall, yellow-leaved bushes. The ground was dry and filled with thorn runlets, but nothing could penetrate the thick pads on Shadic feet.

Jibbawk ducked near a bush and studied it. Its bark was dark red, and there was a cavity inside the bush big enough for him to hide in. He turned and found Maddawk staring.

Maddawk growled and shook like a wet bonpup. His quills swelled out, making tinkling sounds like glass rods. "Get up. You're gonna listen to me, Jibbawk, or I will crush your skull between my claws."

Maddawk was big and filthy, and he stunk of betrayal. He'd gone through the same pod training as Jibbawk and was much stronger. Brute power didn't matter, Jibbawk was faster and in the Shadic world, speed was what really counted. "If you do not want your corpse dragged to Cal-Kaw's feet, you will heed my plan."

"Fine. What are your tacticssss?" Jibbawk hissed.

Maddawk gathered all the Shadics around. One was named Kickawk. He had almost translucent quills and was raised by an alhook of women Shadics. There was Tawk and Velawk. They were sly, tricky brothers and too smart for their own good. The others were inconsequential fools.

Maddawk pointed to Tawk and Velawk. "Flank the outpost, wait for my signal. They've no eyesight for detail when their sun is setting."

"We've no idea where it is," Kickawk whispered, looking around but not tall enough to see over the bushes.

Jibbawk pointed off to his left. "They are over there. These bushes provide cover so any–"

"They need high ground," Maddawk interrupted. "We must surround the outpost and spring

on them."

"What's your signal?" Tawk asked.

"You will hear me call to the wind at the same moment I take out all their guards." Maddawk smiled. "You can have what is left."

The Shadics spread out. They crept from yellow bush to yellow bush, careful not to break twigs or rustle leaves. They were in position before the evening set in.

The outpost was a square building made of clay and putty and had a peaked roof, a wide porch surrounded the building, a guard at each side. Light came from a dozen glowing glass balls hung from the porch eaves connected by a rope.

Ophex

Jibbawk had read about the lights the Ophex used. It fascinated him. He wanted to know how the light went on and off on command and continued to glow even during storms. Most Shadics laughed the magic off as feeble, weak things and didn't give them a second thought. Lanterns in the Shadic world were fueled by oil obtained from the fat of from Fuller Blots and would stay lit even in fierce wind.

The Ophex had powerful magics and were proving difficult to conquer. Their soldiers wore drab gray outfits with lots of pockets, metal cans-like helmets and usually had bandages wrapping their forearms. They had weak, short bodies and snouts with large nostrils like jetmuts.

Jibbawk thought about their objective. They were to bring back some kind of talking box, truly an odd thing for the Resident Ruler to request. Usually, they were to bring back the heads of the Ophex leaders and burn the camp down. Cal-Kaw must be a curious Shadic as well.

Jibbawk will be the one to deliver the box. There was no doubt. If Maddawk initiated the attack, he'd have more kills and a greater opportunity. Jibbawk couldn't let that happen.

He left his position carefully, quietly and cir-

cled around to where Maddawk was supposed to be. Maddawk was not there. Jibbawk backed away and, moving from the cover of the large yellow bushes, found Tawk and Velawk's position a little crowded.

Maddawk was huddled over the brothers whispering. "Jibbawk has taken most of the points in these games. We have no chance of winning by taking one outpost."

"Jibbawk is fast, faster than I've ever seen a Shadic," Tawk said.

"He must not survive this raid. That is our only chance." Maddawk peeked around the bushes, checking his cover. The fool did not look back. "Cal-Kaw and my family go back a long time. He wishes me to win my planet, as do I. If you help me, you will be my second lords."

"What do we do?" Velawk said, nodding, his eyes wide and excited.

"We attack early, from closer positions." Maddawk clenched his fist. "We make sure Jibbawk has no kills, then I will kill him."

"What if he escapes. He has tricks up his sleeve." Tawk said cautiously. It wasn't easy to presume a Shadic plan would fail and not reap consequences.

"Cal-Kaw has given me the locations of very small outposts for us to sack. Either way, I will have the talking box and we will have more of a head count than he could imagine."

Jibbawk backed away, satisfied he knew what to expect. Now was his chance to wreck it.

"Get in position," Maddawk concluded.

Jibbawk slipped away as though he were only the wind. Anger burned inside, growing hotter by the second. He never knew Cal-Kaw supported the Mad family. Jibbawk's mother, Rybawk had once complained that if it weren't for her husband's untimely death, it would have been Jib-ki-bawk that ruled Cicanth and not Cal-Kaw. Could it be that Cal-Kaw paid Maddawk's father to kill Jib-ki-bawk? Could this be the kink in the decades old conspiracy, mouthed by one foul, brutally stupid Shadic?

Jibbawk needed no further evidence. He will win this Testing and take his prize and build a stronger empire than all of Cal-Kaw's lands put together. Then Jibbawk will have his revenge. He smiled as he sneaked to the opposite side of the Ophex outpost. His quills stood on end with pure excitement for the blood he will spill.

Jibbawk settled behind a large bush and craft-

ed his plan. How could he turn Maddawk's plan on its head?

He took a wide leaf from the ground and plucked a small quill from his neck. He jammed the tip into the pad of his finger, right at the base of his thick talon. The blood filled the quill like a pen, and before it dried, Jibbawk scribbled a map on the leaf. The map gave the approximate location of the Shadics surrounding the outpost. Jibbawk then lifted the alanx-binding on his left arm and plucked the longest flalanx. He blew out very drop of poison and threaded the quill through the leaf, so it acted like a wing. Jibbawk had made many of these darts as a child. The right shape and fold of leaf pushed to the back helped the quill fly slower and for a longer distance. He threw it then hid inside one of the yellow bushes.

The quill arched gracefully and hit the soldier just above his collarbone. He dropped his strange, slug-spitting weapon and grabbed the quill. Fear flooded his face, and he fell back, hitting the building wall with a thud. Jibbawk knew the Ophex would think he would die. Normally, the poison would only take a fraction of a second to shut the nervous system down and fill their brains with pain. The soldier stood, confused, pulled the quill out of his skin and noticed the drawing on the leaf.

Immediately, the Ophex pulled a gray box off his waist strap and spoke into it. Jibbawk watched in awe. It was obvious the box would carry the man's voice to other men because a moment later all the soldiers were on high alert and aiming right where the Shadics hid. Curious.

Maddawk attacked early as he planned, while signaling the other Shadics to do the same. He flipped in the air to the porch steps and landed as he released a dozen quills toward the guards. But the guards were ready for him. A soldier aimed a rod at Maddawk. Suddenly, fire burst out of the weapon and engulfed the large shadic. He flailed and tried to flee but was dead in moments.

Kickawk, Tawk and Velawk and the others attacked. They too thought they'd spring on unsuspecting Ophex soldiers but were wrong. Tawk was shot in the shoulder but still got his hand around the throat of a guard. He flung the guard off the porch but his back was ripped apart by slugs from their spitting weapons.

Velawk dodged every shot and successfully stabbed an Ophex soldier in the face, but then suddenly Velawk's head exploded. Someone from inside

the outpost had a slug-spitter, too, and a rather noisy one. The night cracked with a hundred shots.

Kickawk never got to the porch before he was burned alive.

The other useless Shadics died spectacularly when Ophex reinforcements came from the dark, riding on strange, towering beasts that wore heavy metal armor.

The attack only lasted minutes. Bloody heaps of Shadic bodies littered the porch along with only a few Ophex.

Jibbawk huddled inside the bush, watching them speak into their talking boxes. It was amazing to watch their coordination. Shadics simply made loud noises to coordinate. Ophex males held fireless torches and searched the area, each with their own version of slug-spitters.

When they were satisfied of their victory, the soldiers dragged the Shadic bodies to a ditch and burned them.

Jibbawk stayed well hidden, patiently, for an entire day.

The next night he attacked. He alone used the surprise to his advantage, sneaking from one guard to the next, stabbing them in the back. He spun to the front of the building and took out three guards with his poison quills before they could cry out. The porch was clear.

Jibbawk slowly and with care lit the outpost on fire from every angle. The men inside burst from the building where Jibbawk killed them easily.

When all the soldiers were dead, Jibbawk took a deep breath, leaped into the burning building and retrieved the large, metal box from the center table.

There was one more thing to do. Jibbawk went to the pit where the Shadic bodies lay, charred and blackened. He found the massive head of Maddawk and pulled it out of the ashes. Jibbawk placed his claws on either side of Maddawk skull and crushed it, a seemingly perfect response to the dirty beast's earlier threat. Dust filled the air, and Jibbawk breathed it into his lungs. He will do the same to Cal-Kaw someday when the time is right.

A half mile away, Jibbawk found a small clearing and sprinkled Hubbu pollen over his head. He was twisted and sucked through the unstable wormhole, arriving home the only survivor, carrying the talking box and knowing that he would now be granted rule over his very own planet.

Chapter 4
Lan Darr

Jibbawk was ushered in front of ten thousand Shadics of every class, seated on stone seats set in concentric circles surrounding a stage. Jibbawk was showered with coins, trinkets, flowers, quills with fancy designs painted on them and more.

Cal-Kaw and Ixawk stood among the same elders who had been following the Tests. Some glared with narrowed eyes and frowns, but others clapped respectfully.

Cal-Kaw motioned for quiet with his clipped claws. "Jibbawk, you've done remarkably well and have bested all your opponents." Cal-Kaw looked around, mocking the absence of others. "So much so, that you are the only one on this stage now."

Cal-Kaw stood, flipping his shiny black cloak off his shoulders. He picked up the talking box Jibbawk had collected from the outpost and held it high. "We have victory! The other Shadics proved to be so useless; they've chosen to die instead of return." The crowd chanted Jibbawk's name. "We will decode the magic of this talking box so we may use it against our enemies on Nophan. It will be key to removing their power piece by piece, death by death until we rule that planet, shore to shore." The crowd cheered.

Cal-Kaw carefully handed the talking box to an elder and waved him off. "As for our victor. Since you are of Jib-blood and the highest ranking survivor, you will be given your very own planet to rule. The world is called Lan Darr and the local Lan Darrians have been subdued to the point where they will welcome your leadership and rule." The crowd roared. Streamers were thrown, and fire pops exploded in the air. It had been a long time waiting for a Ruler to take Lan Dar.

Ixawk stood and took a golden box from a slave. She opened it slowly like the contents were something vile and dangerous. Inside was a golden scepter, meticulously carved and imbued with gems. She handed it over, bowing her head. "I see how powerful you are and am now below your station."

An old Shadic handed Jibbawk a cape made of the fur of Minacats, blood red, as soft as petals of oa-flowers. A fourth Shadic elder secured golden bands

to Jibbawk's powerful legs. The crowd chanted and stomped. Today would be remembered and Jibbawk would be feared but shown ultimate respect.

Jibbawk held the heavy scepter in his claws and smiled inside. It seemed to vibrate in his clutches but only because Jibbawk's nerves were alive like nests of slithering sertets.

He could see by his peripheral vision that Cal-Kaw was scowling.

Jibbawk strode home, walking tall, through crowds of cheering Shadics and other races brought to Cicanth to be slaves.

Eventually, he passed through the gate that marked his family's sixit of land, leaving the multitudes behind. The gate was a tall arch made of white marble stones with numerous tiles of black relief carvings depicting battle scenes.

His huge family home stood on top of a low hill surrounded by a forest of thin spindet trees. It had a central dome over the main house and a dozen smaller domes over the attachment rooms.

From the woods came a tall Shadic female, gold tape wrapping her arms and thighs and waist. It was Jibbawk's mother, Rybawk, with a six-foot, black blow dart pole resting on her shoulder. She wasn't wearing her cloak or her crown, which didn't surprise Jibbawk. She hated embellishment as much as Shadic females that painted their claws.

"My son, I see you've had success. I wish they let family view the Testings. I would have liked to see your victories." Behind her were two slave Shadics. Slung between them was a mosseater, its blotchy grey fur soaked in blood, head dangling loose. Its chest cavity was already cleaned out and attracting buzzers.

"Ssstill hunting," Jibbawk said. "Why don't you let the sslaves take care of it? You're getting older now."

Rybawk's eyes narrowed. She was tall for a Shadic, but still a foot under her son. Her neck was long and curved back, her shoulders gracefully narrow. She'd painted the tips of her quills green like the moss and had a pack dangling from a thick leather belt for overnight sleeping. "Do you see the size mosseater I bested? He's the largest in the canyon. I chased him a half sixit and I'm not even tired." She pushed past Jibbawk and headed to the house. "Now that you're free, I cannot order you around anymore. I will have to get used to that." She smiled.

"Do you want to join me on my new planet?

It'sss ripe." Jibbawk bowed to the slaves as they passed him, carrying the mosseater to the butcher room. Just a day before, he was their equal; though they were not Jib blood and would never rise to his stature, they were still apart of his clan and he would always appreciate their service.

Rybawk huffed. "You will do better without me." She placed the blow dart pole on clips in a side alcove above razor sharp spears, polished silver lances and decorative swords.

Jibbawk stopped her before she entered the quiet room. "Maddawk said something on Nophan that you must hear."

Her eyes widened. "You know how I feel about the Maddawk bloodline."

"Cal-kaw sss supported him, gave him favor in the final Test. He meant to kill me."

Rybawk kicked, her huge claw smashing through a paper wall, splitting a wood frame. "I knew it. Cal-kaw has been against us since your father's time."

"Did he pay for my father's death?"

"It would seem so." Rybawk pecked Jibbawk's shoulder, hard. Blood pooled on his dark skin. "Now that we know who funds the Maddawk family, those filthy screeches, you must do all you can to seek revenge for our blood line. It is all you will do."

"I plan on it," Jibbawk said without hesitation.

By week's end, Jibbawk and two hundred other Shadics had traveled by Hubbu to the planet Lan Darr. It was a small world where the sun was but a faint dot in the sky, but still bright enough to grow thick forests that would yield good wood. The marble in the mountains was readily accessible, and there was enough of a population so that the Shadics would be well fed.

Jibbawk and the others arrived instantly in a thick forest filled with purplish plants, with bulbous flowers dripping honeydots. Jibbawk ate a flower whole. He breathed in the air of his new possession. It was a perfect world.

Jibbawk looked over a hand-drawn map on a square of dried skin. There were tribes all over Lan Darr, but only one city. It was on the edge of the forest and bordered a harsh desert.

Jibbawk hiked for over an hour before stopping. When he did, it was due to a furry little creature clinging to the side of a thin sapling. The thing stared

in awe; its mouth opened but it didn't make a sound. In one fluid motion, Jibbawk plucked a quill and flung it at the creature, hitting it in the neck. Spasms shook its body for a long moment before it died.

Jibbawk picked up the creature studying it. "Niccce fur. Huge eyes. Thisss odd creature lookssss almosssst intelligent." He tossed it to a slave. "Gut thisss thing and bring it with usss. Sssend out two hunters and find a dozen more for sssupper tonight."

A lower ranked Shadic, obvious by its single arm cuff, nodded and spoke orders to the others. Hunters broke away from the pack as Jibbawk and the main troop continued toward the city.

After a few more hours, Jibbawk arrived at the city the Lan Darrians called Dantia. A wall a hundred feet high built with huge square-cut stones surrounded the city, so Jibbawk could not see in. The wall might stop a pitiful race, but not Shadics. However, it could offer some protection if guarded properly and maybe reinforced with razor sharp barbs. Vines and huge trees grew from the cracks. Jibbawk grabbed a vine and climbed the great wall. Scaling the towering structure was easy, too easy. He'd have to do something about it. Maybe chop the trees down and yank the vines. The outer wall should be as smooth as the

surface of water.

Jibbawk stood at the top, looking into Dantia. Inside was a river delta and a huge sprawl of clay
buildings. Not a single stone structure could be seen.
The wall must be from an ancient civilization because
the current inhabitants looked unexpectedly primitive. Jibbawk was told before his arrival that the locals dealt with farming, fabrics, jewelry, and music,
but not much else. That was going to have to change.

He climbed down the great wall, leaping to

the ground the last fifteen feet. A local Lan Darrian froze in the middle of pulling a net from the main river. Jibbawk strode up to him. The net was filled with squiggly, tentacled creatures. The Lan Darrian stared for a moment then dropped the net and bowed. He was bipedal, large purple colored eyes, wide mouth, smooth black scales speckled with a hit of orange like the very early spike of dawn. This one was thin and wearing a tattered blue coat and skirt.

More Shadics clambered over the great wall and gathered by the fisherman. Jibbawk intentionally left him bowing for a long while, until the creature was visibly shaking.

The Shadic group finally moved on, following the river's edge. There were more fishermen and some females carrying baskets. They were more brightly colored and wore intricate jewelry. They all bowed as Jibbawk passed.

Great fire pits smoldered in the afternoon light. Every pit had a spit for meat to cook on. However, there seemed an air of hunger, desperation, and poverty in Dantia.

The Shadic group headed toward the city center marked by two large mud huts.

Jibbawk was ecstatic. Lan Darr had been set

up perfectly for him.

Night came quickly and bonfires were lit. Jibbawk ate and spoke for a long time with local leaders as they sat near towering flames. Soon, near midnight, three, bright sliver moons rose, delighting the new Shadic ruler.

It took ten years for Jibbawk to set up the capital the way he wanted it. Thousands of various creatures migrated or were imported from different Shadic worlds. He taught the Lan Darrians how to cut marble from the mountains and haul it to Dantia on rolling pallets. With this marble, he built the tallest tower the Lan Darians had ever seen.

At first, the people of Lan Darr were able to do what they pleased. They did not have taxes, rules, regulations or any form of duty forced upon them. Dantia thrived. This was all part of the plan. Slowly, Jibbawk levied taxes, raised a small defense force, and outlawed some annoying local customs like their week-long marriage ceremonies. Still, Danita thrived. Marble buildings were erected, trade with other planets was initiated, and Dantia was flush with food

and coin.

Then came a young teenage boy from a planet called Earth. It was just about the most perfect thing Jibbawk could hope for.

Chapter 5
The Genius from Earth

The day was hot and muggy. Though the sun was hardly visible, the summer day cycles were brighter and the days longer.

Jibbawk sat on his dining throne, cleaning the meat off a small barrit bone— a cute, round animal with a stub nose and flat, grass eating teeth, and the second most delectable dish on Lan Darr. His favorite, and as well as all other Shadics, were the sweet, thick tentacles of the marshid. When paired with a pasty bone-dust sauce, the marshid was at the top of many menus.

The great dining room was the largest in the capital building. It took up most of the first floor, had a towering ceiling that was held up by thick, round pillars of marble. A huge wood table with fifty seats ran the length of the room and at the back was a stairway that twisted up to the second floor. Two oversized wooden doors lead outside and were monitored night and day by Shadic slaves.

A knock echoed in the great hall. The slaves

hefted open one of the doors, letting in a tall, lean Shadic guard.

He stepped inside a couple of feet and bowed.

"Enter into my presenccce," Jibbawk said, licking a claw clean.

"Ruler, we have a gift for you. This one is strange," the guard said.

"Bring in thisss gift. Do not keep your ruler wanting."

The guard made a whistling noise. Two shad-ics dragged in a short, mostly hairless creature that looked as afraid as a startled grass-eater.

Jibbawk had never seen such a pink being. It had dull, loose fitting clothes and very odd feet coverings. He approached the creature cautiously. It was clean; that much he liked. Jibbawk reached out and grabbed its thick, dark hair and tugged its head back. The creature's eyes became very moist and leaked water. It seemed like it wanted to call out, but it didn't. Jibbawk leaned close and sniffed its scent, pressing his beak to the creature's cheek. It seemed so weak and vulnerable, yet there was something about it that fascinated Jibbawk.

"Leave us," Jibbawk ordered the guards. The guards left, the slaves closing the door behind them.

Jibbawk dragged the creature by its arm to the table and sat it down. He returned to his plate and continued to eat.

Jibbawk knew what it was about the creature that fascinated him. It was similar to the Ophex peoples. Their clothes were cut evenly, the stitching a perfect pattern along the seams just like this pink creature's clothing. They had strange foot coverings, too. Like their feet were too weak to step on the ground and not become damaged.

The creature's head barely rose above the lip of the table. It was lean and not very muscular. It had a thin patch of hair on its chin.

After a long while, the creature looked around. It obviously studied the room. It eyed the piles of food on the table, the towering marble columns, the windows lined with wire mesh and the fabric tapestries the Lan Darrians gave to Jibbawk.

The creature spoke in an unfamiliar language, its voice quivering, "Wer e am?" it said. "Pliz ta mi om. No Ert an a mor?"

It was a strange language, but its articulation was clear and precise. It was one of the only languages that didn't annoy Jibbawk upon first exposure. Jibbawk had learned Lan Darr's local language years ago, but the grunts and subtle throat inflections were stupid and untenable, and the locals were having a hard time with Jibbawk's native language.

Jibbawk stood and walked down the long table to the creature. He picked up a stone from the floor and set it on the table. He pointed to it then to the creature's mouth.

"R..rock," the creature said, its voice quivering.

Jibbawk smacked the table.

"T...table."

Jibbawk patted the creature's chest almost knocking it over.

"Ricky Boldary," Ricky coughed out.

Was the thing male? Or female? Awfully weak for a male.

Jibbawk focused his energy on learning Ricky's very simple language and like anything he set his mind to, he learned it fast.

Ricky was from a planet called Earth, roughly fourteen years old and lived in a city called Erie, Pennsylvania. The Earthling quickly became Jibbawk's new curiosity, like a fun pet.

Months later, Jibbawk, Ricky, and the same

female slave Jibbawk had meet during his Testing lounged under a huge, colorful canopy on the tall roof of his capital building, overlooking Dantia. She was a rare breed of Shadic, her eyes more orange than red, her quills short and striped instead of dark brown. She still wore the black tape of failure over her arms, but Jibbawk liked her so much, he let the rest of her remain unwrapped. He disregarded her given name and called her Jib-Selawk.

Ricky watched a narrow, wooden boat traverse the rivers.

"Dantia looks like a place on Earth called Venice," Ricky said. The boy's collared shirt and khaki pants were kept clean, but starting to become threadbare.

"Is Veniccccce near Erie?" Jibbawk asked the boy. He was draped over a lounge seat next to the female who was delicately cleaning Jibbawk's quills with her long and sharp beak.

"No, but I saw pictures in books. We have all kinds of books on Earth. Don't you read?"

"We passss down our traditions by training and tutorship," Jibbawk said.

"I had lots of textbooks with me when I came here. I had a chemistry book, a history book, a one on new maths, oh and an English book, too. I know lots of stuff. People say I'm a genius, but I just remember stuff. When I read something, its sticks in my brain."

Jibbawk sat up. "And are there books you have not read?"

"Ya tons more. I'm only a sophomore. My teachers let me skip my entire freshman year because of how much I've read. But there's a lot I don't know. If you want to see some of my books you'll have to find my book bag. When you captured me, I dropped it in the river." Ricky came back from the edge and sat just outside the shade. His species must love soaking up the heat. Ricky looked at his hands and cleaned grime from under his fingernails. "I was on my way to school when I saw the Hubbu flower. There was one on the side of the road. It was so big I had to pick it. I have this girl, you see. She was waiting for me to walk her to class."

"Tell me exactly where you left your bag." Jibbawk listened to Ricky and called a guard over. "Find the pack and do not come back to Dantia until you have it."

The guard nodded and left.

"So you are a sssmart Earthling, huh?" Jibbawk mused.

"Yup." Ricky leaned back, his arms behind his head resting on a large pillow made of stone beads so Shadic quills could not destroy it. "What about the Shadic Empire? There aren't very many of you here."

"The Shadic empire has explored thirty planets, ten of which are ruled by Shadic masters," Our race is ten thousand years old." Jibbawk let Jib-Selawk clean his quills. "Our culture is guarded by tightly controlled rules and customs, but I fear they are becoming obsssolete. The Ophex on Nophan have magics I do not understand but offer a disstinct advantage. Also, your Earth sseems to have some of these abilities as well. I've heard of many cultures and customs but by far Earth has the most intriguing ones." Jibbawk reflected on all the time he'd spent talking with Ricky. When the boy first stopped crying, fidgeting incessantly, and staring with fear at every Shadic that passed, he opened up to his new place and was a pleasure to talk to. The wealth of knowledge he had was as valuable as all the gold in the galaxy to Jibbawk.

"Tell me more about Earth," Jibbawk said— his favorite discussion of late.

"The year is nineteen fifty-one. We're only six years from the war. My pa died in France, but my ma took care of us pretty good. She sewed for a tailor downtown and I was a janitor at our local library at night while going to school during the day."

Jibbawk waved away the topic. "Yessss, yesss, no more about your mother or your day job. What about the war." Jibbawk looked over Ricky's thin, small frame. "How does your kind fight?"

"Guns, bombs, planes, tanks," Ricky said. He explained what all these things were. Ophexians had guns. Jibbawk had called them slug-spitters. He'd seen first-hand what the gun's true power was.

"But what really helped us win was that we decoded the Nazi secret messages. We knew where they were and how they were going to fight. We spoke a language from a tribe called Navajos, and the Axis Powers couldn't break our code. They could listen to our radio transmissions all day and not know what we were gonna do."

"What are these radios?"

"We can speak into devices, or boxes, that carry our voices across the Earth. It would come out of another, similar device."

Jibbawk nearly fell out of his seat. "Talking boxes," he muttered. Now he was getting somewhere.

"Never heard of radio waves before, huh? Do you have any other types of technology?" Ricky asked. "Other than building huge marble towers?"

Jibbawk nodded. "We have some powerful means. We know math and use the skies and stars like clocks. We know how to melt metals, make ropes and shape wood. We know how to build strong buildings out of stone. But there is much we don't know. There are Ophexians on Nophan that have talking metal boxes and weapons that spit slugs and poles that shoot fire. But they are ultimately weaker than we are."

Jibbawk chuckled, his brain musing on his own culture. "We have magic, too." He cleaned a quill with his beak. "There are many plants and animals that give us abilities. Slithan bones give us strength and reduce joint pain; rut leaves can give usss energy for days, and there are rumors there are beetles that can make usss immortal."

"Really," Rickys' eyebrows lifted up. "How does beetle do that?"

Jibbawk shrugged. "It is one of our oldest ssstories. Some think it is false, but I believe it is real. Once we find the beetle, we will not be stopped. Shadics will rule the galaxy for forever more." Ricky folded his arms and turned away.

"Tell me more about Earth," Jibbawk ordered.

Cal-Ka would be impressed with Jibbawk's new pet. He had to be careful, though. Cal-Ka would have the authority to take Ricky if he pleased and that simply could not happen.

Chapter 6
Rise of the Jibbawk
Referendum

Jibbawk and Ricky spent the next year learning all about Earth technology, including radios, motors, planes and the purpose of schools and libraries. Jibbawk had scribes copy Ricky's textbooks over and over and deliver them into the hands of Shadics around the planet.

But the information wasn't complete. Jibbawk intended to learn all about the 'talking boxes' but was having a hard time understanding what radio waves were. Even after flipping over the dining table and kicking a slow cooked carcass of a barrit across the great dining hall, he still couldn't comprehend frequency.

That night Jibbawk sat near the grand fire pit in the center of town. The celebration was for Jibbawk's eleventh year as ruler of Lan Darr, but no matter how many drinks he downed, nothing could improve his mood. He wasn't learning quickly enough. He looked over to his capital building. Oil lamps lit up the windows in a pleasing pattern that rose into the sky. The building was still the tallest in the Dantia, but not by far. It should be bigger, taller and with more windows.

One of the dancers twirled up to Jibbawk, trying to dance in front of him. Her dark scales gleamed in the firelight; the edges flared with a touch of red. Though she wore the finest silk sashes and brightest ribbons and they flew around her in fantastic swirls, Jibbawk wanted her out of his sight. She blocked the view of his capital building, disrupting his thoughts, agitating the soil into swirls of choking dust. He didn't care about her curves or the painted symbols on the more delicate scales. He shooed her away, but she only draped the end of her sash into his lap and got closer. She was weak and distracting him!

Jibbawk's heart seized like it had sprung a beaga trap. He leaped to his feet and snatched the female's sash. She yelped, caught completely off guard. Jibbawk ripped the sash off and pushed her. She flew back and landed in the tall bonfire, screaming. Sparks flew in a thousand directions, and burning timber topped outward. Shadics and Lan Darrians

leaped away from the rupturing fire and embers, but many were pelted and burned. The music stopped, replaced by shouting, crying and panic.

Jibbawk turned from the chaos, noticing Ricky hiding behind a wide log bench, the boy's mouth open and his eyes wide. Jibbawk looked up to the three sliver moons that graced Lan Darr's night skies. He listened to the confusion and blubbering behind him then marched back to the capital. He thrust a claw at Ricky and gestured for him to follow. Jibbawk and a detachment of six guards left the celebrations in ruins.

Jibbawk locked Ricky in his room then stomped up the six flights of stairs to his office. The oil lamp sconces were too bright for his mood so as he passed them; he snuffed them out. Jibbawk kicked open the door to his office. It was a secure room without windows. Tall cabinets filled with scrolls lined the walls, surrounding a large desk.

Jibbawk stomped into the room, caught off guard by his most trusted advisor, Halawk. Halawk sat at a desk stamping approvals on construction requests and travel papers. He was older and had known Jibbawk since hatching. Every quill on Halawk was pinned down or plucked, and his beak was clipped. He'd been ruler of Cataheen for fifty years, had conquered five off-world races and survived three coup attempts. He was the only Shadic Jibbawk considered smarter than he was. Tonight, he was wearing a black, patchwork cloak made from the skins of a dozen rare palrats.

Halawk turned and set down his ink quill. His eyes weren't as sharp red as they had been, but his vision still acute. "Something troubling you?"

"Time." Jibbawk turned from his alcove door and instead paced. He pulled his red fur cloak off his back, threw his golden helmet to the wall and pulled his arm cuffs off. "Ahhh, sssometimes these things I wear feel sssso oppressssive." He flexed his muscles, and all his quills stood on end. It easily doubled his apparent size. Slaves were not allowed in the ruling office, so the attire remained on the floor.

Halawk's voice was raspy. "Your energy is to be expected. I was once in your place, impatient, dreamy, foolish." Halawk picked up the quill, dipped it in ink and continued signing papers. "It will pass."

"Lan Darr can be more powerful than Cicanth," Jibbawk spat.

Halawk set down the quill again and turned in his chair. "And how do you propose to accomplish

this grand idea? Cicanth is an old society. Ruled by Shadics for hundreds of years."

Jibbawk continued pacing. "Cicanth is stuck in its ways. Dantia's growth is fasster by far. He tapped his massive talons on the stone floor. "I need more Earth technology. The boy from Earth only has four books. Though his mathss are phenomenal and I'm hearing amazing things from the chemistss, the others are not much usse right now."

"Then you must go to Earth." Halawk's eyes focus tightly on Jibbawk. "Take a raiding party. Kill whoever you see and bring back what you can."

Jibbawk shook his head. "No, Ricky knows what we need. I would be blind on Earth. Plus, they are much more advanced than even the Ophex. And we're having a tough time conquering them as it is. No, I do not wish to alert any Earthling to Hubbu travel."

"Then why not send the boy back?"

"Yess, I have thought about thiss." Jibbawk walked to the window and breathed the cool night air. "There is no connection here. He would never return."

"Then connect him here. You've told me how sentimental Earthlings can be. Make him a family here. Go to Earth, capture a female and bring her back. Use the female as leverage, so he will do your bidding."

Jibbawk's eyes narrowed, and his mind raced. "Yess. Oncce there is someone here he does not want me to hurt, I can ssend him to Earth whenever I wish and have him retrieve the correct bookss for me."

Jibbawk picked up his cloak, his helmet, and Alanx-bindings and took them to his sleeping alcove. Finally, he had the answers he sought. His mind stopped its incessant spinning and set out to devise great possibility.

Jibbawk slept in fits. Visions of electricity, of guns, of radios and war filled his mind. He would be the one to take Ophex down. It will be his satellite kingdom. Shadic law allowed a conqueror two satellite worlds. More than that, it was said that maintaining power was too foolish to attempt. Jibbawk would change that to three worlds. After taking over the Ophex on Nophan, he would turn his sight to Cicanth and Cal-kaw.

Finally, after giving up on sleep, altogether he dressed and stomped to Ricky's room.

Ricky popped up, fear filling his pale face. "Wha—"

"I want to learn more about this electric-ity you ssspeak of. Will you be able to retrieve the booksss I need to learn thisss?" Jibbawk asked. "It seems like the best technology to master firsst."

Ricky rubbed his eyes. "Y. . . yes. I can get you any kind of book you want. The library I worked at has a million books." Though Ricky had seemed asleep, he didn't look like he had gotten a wink of it. The boy couldn't look Jibbawk in the eye.

"What is wrong with you?" Jibbawk asked, though he didn't care about the feelings of others, Ricky was essential to his plans. He had to keep the boy from Earth healthy and happy.

"I'm fine. I just— you just pushed the woman into the fire," Ricky's voice cracked into a high pitch. He cleared his throat and stared at his fingers, trying to stifle his shaking hands.

Jibbawk ground his beak together as he sup-pressed his irritation. "I will apologize to the family and give them a half a bitix of land for restitution. Fair enough?"

Ricky nodded then looked at Jibbawk. "That's a start."

Jibbawk spun on his clawed feet. "Mind how you speak to your ruler, young Ricky. You do not want my wrath," Jibbawk said casually. Ricky nodded as Jibbawk stomped out of the room, locking the door behind him. If Ricky were any other creature, he'd have cut his throat.

When the morning came, Jibbawk had his plan all worked out. There were as many Hubbu colors as the rainbow, and every colored pollen went to a different planet. Lan Darrian's did not cultivate the color Hubbu that went to Earth. He would have to search Lan Darr to find it. Ricky had said the color was a bright orange.

Jibbawk took a bag and loaded it with food and water. He included a pair of shackles that would fit the small wrists of a human. Going to Earth will be so extremely dangerous, the only Shadic that could do the job right was him.

Before he left on his quest for the orange Hubbu flower, Jibbawk set a few things in motion.

"Triple the taxes on all of Dantians. I want to pile up so much gold and jewels it will ssspill out the windows of my capital building. It will be my referendum. Let the people know it is to build the greatest city in the galaxy."

Halawk was taking notes. "About time we raised taxes," he grumbled.

Jibbawk continued. "I want fifty more Shadics and over a hundred more Lan Darrians learning English and at least twenty more memorizing the textbooksss we have. I will return when I've obtained a gift for our young Ricky."

Jibbawk took his meager bag and headed out of the capital building. He glided down the five flights of stairs like he was floating. He'd been waiting for this momentum to kick start his agenda. It turned out that all he needed was to push some slimy dancer into the flames for him to catch fire.

Chapter 7
Ricky's Gift

It took Jibbawk a month to find the orange Hubbu flower. He hiked down narrow valleys between two-thousand-foot cliffs, crossed the valley of sinkholes, swam the river Digonie to get to the tangled Kape Forest. He wasn't tired or frustrated; it was simply the task at hand.

The day he found the flower he was looking for firewood. It had been a long day of hacking through mossy tangles that rendered Kape mostly impassable. It was an irritating forest; the thick canopy of sharp-smelling green leaves was occupied by shriek-birds and loonie begits who threw things at passersby as a form of entertainment. A cacophony of sounds surrounded Jibbawk, disturbing him. He was not looking forward to trying to rest while these creatures hooted and shrieked like madmen.

Jibbawk took his firewood bundle back to a clearing he'd found. It was a muddy patch of dirt that would serve as his bed for the night. The edges of the clearing were occupied with purple fen bushes and the pyramid flowers so common on Lan Darr.

Jibbawk ripped out handfuls of grass and leaves and made a pillow.

The day grew late and the sky began its slow decent to darkness, encouraging the animals to become more raucous. Jibbawk looked around, quill in hand ready to spear any noisy animal that came within twenty feet.

Instead, his eyes spied something beyond a nearby spindly bush. *Orange!* The color was inside the hollow of an ancient tree stump. Jibbawk jumped onto an adjacent log, holding his breath and tempering his expectations. Sure enough, there was an orange Hubbu flower, soaking up whatever remained of the sparse sunlight.

Jibbawk carefully plucked the flower. It was as large as a dinner plate, all Hubbu blooms were. Tiny, glassy leaves surrounded the enormous bulb of pollen in the middle. Jibbawk marveled at the power the little plant held. It, too, decided in its evolution that the whole galaxy was for the taking and it took it. The plant wasn't satisfied with inhabiting just the world it was born in, so it spread itself across a hundred others. Such a fluke of nature, a beautiful fluke.

Jibbawk marked his location on the map and

continued his search. He easily found another orange Hubbu growing out of the crook where one tree split into two.

Without delay, he scraped the pollen into a stone vial, careful not to agitate it too much, and stoppered the top. Quick movement and turbulent air ignited the reaction that opened the wormhole across space. He tucked the vial into his bag where he kept a supply of blue pollen; that would bring him home.

Jibbawk scraped the last of the orange dusty substance into the bottom curvature of his forefinger claw and held it over his head. With a twist of his wrist, the pollen cascaded around him. The door to Earth opened, and Jibbawk was sucked through. Space twisted around him like a vortex, pain flooded his body, and darkness overtook him.

Seconds later, Jibbawk was spat out of thin air and landed among tall, thick-stalked plants–not as tall as he was, but only his head was above them. They were planted in neat rows and extended as far as the eye could see. The sun was directly overhead and hot. Jibbawk squinted and recoiled from the ball of fire in the sky. He had forgotten what a sun looked and felt like.

Motion from his left startled Jibbawk, and he crouched. Something loud came his way. He peeked over the tall stalks. It was a metal car on wheels but looked nothing like the cars in Ricky's school book. Jibbawk waited and watched. It fascinated him. The loud machine had immense wheels and a scoop in the front. It pushed on two rows of the plant, cut the stocks and forced the it into a bin where it disappeared. It was like a great, green beast. Somewhere inside the metal body it processed the plant and spat unused pulp out of a side pipe. Jibbawk could see one human driving the machine and not a single picker anywhere on the field. On any given farm on Lan Darr or any other field in the Shadic Empire, harvest time employed hundreds of slaves, thousands, all at an immense cost. Everyone had to be housed, fed, clothed. If only he had some of these huge 'cars.'

Jibbawk ducked again and moved quickly in the opposite direction. Back to the task at hand. He needed to find a female for the boy so he could control him.

Jibbawk arrived at the end of the field and peeked. It was a road. He couldn't risk traveling out in the open, so he stayed in the cover of the plants, following the road. It wasn't easy moving through the

thick stalks, but there was little choice.

A human's voice pricked the tiny quills in Jibbawk's ear holes. He got as low as he could. Two humans walked the side of the road; both appeared much younger than Ricky, and they were boys. Jibbawk let them pass and continued his quest. The farther down the road, he went, the more people he had to stop for. So much so that Jibbawk slunk a few more rows deeper into the field and lay on his belly. He ripped out some plants and covered himself with them. It was a good thing this crop was so dense. It was the best place to hide and wait for the perfect female for Ricky.

Jibbawk let the sun go down. When it was sufficiently dark, he moved on. It was more pleasant to creep in the shadows; it reminded Jibbawk of the basement under his parents huta, where lettix fruit was dried and cured. It had to be kept hot and dark, and Jibbawk was kept there when he misbehaved as a young pek. He embraced the dark and the poisonous sictas and the sour, humid odors.

Jibbawk maneuvered through the tough plants until he came to a small house off the side of the road. No, not a house, a bar. Shadic cities had similar establishments. Inside were hundreds of males and females. He waited at the edge of the field, watching the humans come and go.

The night grew late. Jibbawk was about to move on when the bar's door flew open, and a man stumbled through it, hanging onto a woman. She wore a long yellow dress that billowed at her waist like a bell. Her dark brown hair was tied into a bun, and she carried a small black bag slung over her shoulder.

The man moved to the driver side of an older truck. "I'm fine, darlin'. I can drive juss fine."

The two opened the squeaky doors and got inside. Jibbawk smiled. This man would be easy to take out and the woman easy to capture.

The couple started arguing, then the woman screamed. She kicked open the door and ran. The guy wrestled himself out his door and followed her. He stumbled in the dirt and fell. The woman circled around another car and headed back to the truck. She leaned in and pulled out a long slug-spitter. Ricky called them guns.

Jibbawk was thoroughly entertained.

She spun around and lifted the rifle up just as the man came at her. When he saw the gun, his eyes lit up like two little stars, and he fell over.

"I'm not some cheap girl you can take advantage of," she snapped. "We're through. You hear me!"

"Pu the shotgun down, less talk about this," the man said, swaying.

"Give me the truck keys; you're walking it off," She ordered.

He shook his head. "Naw-ta-chance." He was getting angry.

She clicked the shotgun hammer back and raised it. The barrel was shorter than the guns the Ophex used, but it was just as deadly. "Get outta here, then. I don't need your rust-bucket truck."

The man blubbered a response, but eventually got in his truck and drove off. Jibbawk was not used to females overruling men. It would seem that that gun negated the strength the man had over her.

The female, holding the shotgun across her chest, started walking down the road. Jibbawk followed from the cover of the corn field. But it was tough to keep up with her and remain silent.

She stopped and aimed the gun into the corn. Jibbawk crouched.

"Who's there?" she asked. Her bun had come loose, and her hair hung around her neck in tangled curls. "If that's you, Billy, I will blow a hole through your leg so fast. Don't think I won't!"

Jibbawk plucked a quill and zeroed in on her chest. His nerves twitched as he aimed.

She looked terrified of the darkness, but didn't run, displaying an astonishing strength for a female. Jibbawk held his quill and watched. If she pulled the trigger, he might be hit. He knew he could still take her down with a quill to the neck, but being shot would ruin his plans. A subordinate would fall prey to this type of impatience. Jibbawk was more careful, more thoughtful. Ophex guns tore open the other Shadics during his Testing. The weapons were powerful enough to give any intelligent being pause. He lowered the quill and took a calming breath. One sign of an intelligent ruler is knowing when force becomes counterproductive.

"I'm not Billy," Jibbawk said in a clear and unmistakable voice. "I'm here to look for sssome-one that can help me." He remained in the shadows, knowing his appearance and height will startle the female.

"Who are you?" she asked, keeping the gun pointed into the field. "This shotgun is fully loaded and I've got more shells in my purse, so don't you try a thing."

"I'm from another planet called Lan Darr." Jibbawk paused to see how she took the statement.

The female huffed, "You been readin' too many pulp fictions." Her tone hardened. "I don't like this game."

"Not a game," Jibbawk said in his most diplomatic voice. "A human found his way to my planet and taught me ssssome English. His name is Ricky Boldary. He's in trouble now, and only another human can help him."

"Come out of the corn so I can see you," the female demanded. "If you're some kid playing one of his comic characters, I'll have your father string you up." Her voice quivered, and her grip on the gun tightened. She stepped back, now almost in the middle of the road.

Jibbawk stood slowly. His head rose above the corn.

Her jaw dropped, and she took another step back. "You... you... you got some nerve, scarin' a girl... in a costume... like that." She gasped for breath.

Jibbawk held out his arms and stepped out of the shadows. He could see her body rocking with fear, so he dropped to one knee. "Do not be afraid of me. I'm assssking you to come with me and help your fellow human. He is a fourteen-year-old boy. Around your age, I think. You will be enchanted by the beauty of Lan Darr. And it is sssafe as long as you are with me."

She aimed into the air and fired a shot. The quiet night split like a crack of thunder tore through it. A dozen sleeping ravens in the cornfield startled awake and flew off. "Get outta here, whoever you are." Her eyes were wide and shimmering with tears.

Jibbawk stepped toward her, arms still out. "He needs help, now. I will return you to Earth no later than one week from today."

"Not a chance, creep!" She re-aimed at Jibbawk's chest and backed down the road toward the bar, keeping the gun on Jibbawk. "Help!" she screamed. "Someone!" Her pace quickened.

Jibbawk rolled his eyes, his patience vanished. He flung the quill at her then flipped into the air. The quill nailed the exposed skin just above her collar bone. She screamed and pulled the trigger.

The female doubled over in pain, her scream lasting only a moment. She passed out, falling on the road, clocking her head.

Jibbawk lunged at her, snatched the quill out of her neck and tossed it aside. His shoulder regis-

tered pain and blood tickled his follicles. He had been shot. There were five or six punctures around his shoulder, small and scattered.

Two men came out of the bar. "Hello?" one called out.

Jibbawk, smiling at the minuscule amount of pain the shot caused, opened the bag he'd kept dangling off his shoulder and took out the blue pollen vial. Orange took him to Earth, but would not return him home. Blue would open the wormhole to Lan Darr; he had plenty. He pinched some of the pollen in his clawed fingers. With his free hand, he carefully put the vial back in his bag and slung it over his shoulder.

The men called out, looking for whoever had screamed. Jibbawk had to hurry. More men came from the bar, swarming the parking lot.

Jibbawk hung the shotgun on his shoulder. One of the men ran to the road. He saw Jibbawk and the female. "Mitch, over here," he called out. "Hey, man," the man said. "What you doin' there?" He ran toward Jibbawk, only two-hundred-feet away or so.

Jibbawk lifted the female off the ground and, with great care, held her under his arm. He didn't need any more quills to poke her delicate skin. Too much poison would kill her. He stood, raising up to his nine-foot-height.

The man running at him stopped, gawking. "Holy, mother of…"

Jibbawk spun the hand with the pollen over his head, releasing it. It cascaded around him, and the sparks exploded, connecting like electric spider webs and drew open the wormhole.

Chapter 8
The Hustle

Jibbawk arrived on Lan Darr as dawn colored the sky velvety blue. He was near the river Digonie, the main source of water for Dantia, leading right to the city. Jibbawk figured he was only five miles away and it pleased him. Hubbu travel was very unpredictable and could have landed him in the Deadlands or on top of the two-thousand-foot cliffs.

He laid the female down and searched for a victus tree. He found one an hour later and scraped off huge sections of its bark. Victus wood burned bright red and would signal Jibbawk's army to his location.

He started a fire with twigs and kindling. When it was tall and burning bright, he set the victus tree bark on top. The fire lit the sap, and red smoke poured into the sky. The smoke was sweet, and Jibbawk breathed it in, letting it relax him. He had his prize for Ricky.

Now he planned to set the next part of his

plan in motion.

Jibbawk took out his water pouch and drank deeply. He found a rock to lean on and took a deep breath. His shoulder hurt, but the small amount of blood coming from the wound wasn't enough to worry him.

The female woke up with a start. She clutched the small wound on her neck and screamed loud and long, startling even the worms in the soil.

Jibbawk remained reclined on the rock.

The female scooted backward, smashing grass. She got to her feet, seeing she was surrounded by purple pyramid plants and spotted tang trees and paused. White, fuzzy flowers floated lazily along, more kicked up by her movement. The Digonie River sped past, blocking any escape.

She spun to face Jibbawk, picked up a large rock and threw it at him. The rock bounced harmlessly off his chest. "What are you?" she cried out, picking up another rock and throwing it, missing him entirely. She burst into tears and fell to her knees. "Leave me alone, you monster."

"Think of me as you wish. I've a job to do. What I told you was very near the truth. Ricky Boldary is here, and he needs you."

"Take me home. My father and his brothers will find you and kill you," she said through tears. Jibbawk let her cry for as long as she needed. The female gathered her yellow dress into a ball and squeezed the fabric. Her hands were bleeding, probably cut by the sharp blades of grass.

"Ricky needs companionship," Jibbawk said easily.

She spat at him. "I'm not some prize you can give away." She lunged, grabbed a thick branch and ran at Jibbawk. He leaped to his feet, snatched the branch from her hands and pushed her back. She fell on her butt, crying out again.

Jibbawk stood tall, towering over her, his quills rising and doubling his apparent size. "You and Ricky can go home, but only onccce I have what I want. Until then, you will do as you are told or I'll sssink another quill into your ugly pink sssskin. Another shot in the neck and you go blind, deaf and paralyzed. Too much and you die. I'll get another female for Ricky. Am I making myssself clear?"

The female touched the wound on her neck. Her chin quivered, "Oh God. . ."

Jibbawk leaned close, "On this planet, I am your God."

She rolled back, curling into a ball on the dirt, and cried again.

An hour later a dozen Shadic soldiers and a handful of slaves found Jibbawk and the female and escorted them to a long wooden boat, with a fabric canopy and four-oar stations on either side. The front bow was intricately carved into animal shapes and rose high above the boat. The female was more calm and took orders easily, though she was still shaken and full of fear. Jibbawk found it amusing that she glanced longingly at the swords hung over the soldiers' shoulders and the daggers at their waist belts.

The slaves rowed to Dantia, passing through the towering wall that had been there before Jibbawk's arrival and slowly made their way to the capital building.

The female didn't say a word. In fact, she was quite fascinated by the planet, Dantia, the canals and the local scaled inhabitants Allan had described as looking like salamanders. Jibbawk let her soak it all in. He was proud of the progress Dantia had made in the last ten years. The buildings were twice as tall, the canals reinforced with huge bricks and concrete. Stone bridges spanned the waterways, and the colors

of Jibbawk's royal bloodline topped every building and shop. As Jibbawk passed his people, they bowed deeply and remained there until Jibbawk was out of sight.

Jibbawk tried to help the female out of the boat, but she recoiled. He let her get out by herself and then lead her up the marble steps and through the massive doors of the capital building. It took two slaves just to open them.

Ricky was at the far end of the enormous, polished wood table, bending over papers and speaking to Halawk. Ricky looked up and stared.

Jibbawk took the female's arm and held her facing Ricky. "You have done great work for me. Your sssservice is indispensssable. I present you with thissss gift."

Jibbawk forced her down. "To your knees," he hissed under his breath.

Ricky blinked dumbly as the girl reluctantly got down.

Halawk nodded and smiled to Jibbawk. "I will leave you to your gift, young Ricky." He gathered up the papers and walked away.

"Uh, but," Ricky stuttered. His cheeks were an unusual shade of red, and he blinked furiously.

"I've also awarded you the entire basement as a home for you and your bride." Jibbawk looked at a guard. "Take them down and let them get acquainted."

The guard took the two humans to the basement and locked them inside.

Jibbawk rested peacefully, a job well done.

The next day he woke and was at breakfast before the cooks had time to finish cooking. He waited, patiently. Halawk came down as the servants were filling the table up with caka eggs, oap skins, and marshid tentacles. "How are the taxes coming? Are the collectors experiencing any disobedience?"

"Not a single incident," Halawk said as he sat next to Jibbawk. His plate was set before him and his goblet filled with yola juice. He slurped up the tentacle of a marshid cooked in red pip sauce. "Revenue is way up. By this time next year, we shall have enough to build our invasion force."

Jibbawk nodded and ate a chunk of fried oap skin. "And about teaching more to read the English?"

"Enthusiasm is high, unexpectedly so. More than three hundred have signed up to learn to read and write. They're finding the language entirely more dynamic and expressive. Thousands have signed up

to attend the metal and mining initiative. Ricky's book helped us to identify and successfully reproduce what Earthlings called steel." Halawk continued, "We've also found sources of saltpeter and coal. Together they make the gunpowder."

Jibbawk stopped chewing. "Yes, this is good. Very good."

"This black chalky rock Ricky's book calls coal." Halawks eyes lit up. "It burns hot and for such a long time. It's similar to the peat we'd been using from the dried-up marshland but much better. Three mines are being dug, and they're rich with the coal."

"Ricky has his female. I will now use her as leverage. The two will bond for a week or so before I take Ricky to Earth. Together we will bring back every book we need to conquer the Ophex." Jibbawk's eyes gleamed. He popped a fried oap into his mouth and chewed happily. He didn't dare say it to Halawk, but once Ophex was conquered, he will use his advanced army on Cal-kaw and revenge his father's untimely death.

A Moon cycle passed. The business of Dantia ran predictably like the motion of the stars.

One bright morning Jibbawk glided down the steps with a powerful feeling inside him. He pleasantly ordered his breakfast from the nearest slave, who'd been rehanging a tapestry after cleaning it, and moved to the basement steps. He was about to descend them when he heard Ricky and Elinor speaking.

"I like you," Elinor said. "You're so funny and smart. You're a genius!" She laughed.

"I like you, too. More than any girl I've known." The was a pause. "I'm sorry we're stuck here, but I'll try and ask Jibbawk again to let you go home."

"I know you're trying. Don't get into trouble," she said. "How do you like my new dress?"

Another pause. "It's amazing. You're changing the style of this whole planet. Did you know that? You're making history here."

She giggled.

Jibbawk didn't want to lose his appetite by listening to them chitter any longer so he retreated to the dining table. He dinned in ardor, fattening his stomach on delectable marshid tentacles and a mountain of neps and oap skin.

After breakfast, Jibbawk summoned Ricky to the great dining table. Ricky entered, followed by the two guards who shadowed him wherever he went. Ricky bowed to Jibbawk.

Jibbawk motioned for him to sit. "How is your new bride? Is she behaving?"

Ricky shrugged. "On Earth, we don't pick our brides like this." He picked at his fingernails. "But she's cute and smart."

"I do not care what you do with her. She will keep you company any way you sssee fit." Jibbawk waited for the servants to bring out Ricky's books and the stacks of notes Jibbawk used to learn to write. "Now, let's continue our writing lessons."

"Can you let her go home?" Ricky asked.

"No," Jibbawk said plainly.

"I . . . I feel sorry for her. She's missing her family. I am too, but, I've gotten past it. I really like helping your race out. I know I'll see my family again. You've always kept your word with me. But she's scared."

"I do not care for her fear. Overcoming it will make her strong. She is already a very fierce female. I watched her overpower her previous husband and almost kill him." Ricky let Jibbawk explain how he met her.

"It's just not right," Ricky finally said. The boy was pushing his tongue.

Jibbawk took a deep breath. Appeasing Ricky

was so difficult sometimes. If Ricky weren't so important to his war effort, he'd have his head removed
and burned. "Fine. I need you to go to Earth and
collect as many booksss as you can. I want to know
about these 'cars,' about factories, about guns and
ships and airplanes. I want to develop this electricity
you speak of, and I want to learn what this radio can
do for me. So I will keep her here for one week. You
will go to Earth and collect these things for me, and
she will remain unharmed."

Ricky pounded the table. "You can't hurt her!"

Jibbawk stood. His anger startled Ricky so
much he fell off his chair.

"You do not speak to me that way, creature
from Earth. I will send a thousand Shadic hunters to
your planet and destroy everything we touch. They
will bring this knowledge to me one way or the other." Jibbawk steadied himself and sat. "But I would
rather do this in a more productive way. Now sit back
down."

Ricky grabbed the chair and got off the floor.
He sat, clutching his wrist. "Just don't hurt her," he
mumbled.

"I give you my word as the ruler of Lan Darr."

Chapter 9
The Great Accumulation

Jibbawk and Ricky traveled back to Earth twelve times in three weeks. Ricky had behaved well and followed orders perfectly, knowing his actions kept the female captive safe. Information flooded Lan Darr, lifting off a great and primitive veil of ignorance.

On the first trip, Ricky took Jibbawk to the small library Ricky cleaned for money. The boy used a key on his ring to unlock the door. Jibbawk ducked into the library, hitting his head on the low doorway. The smell of books was strong. Jibbawk moved into the darkness, breathing deep. "Sssuch a pleasant odor."

Ricky flicked on the lights. Jibbawk gawked at the sheer number of books on the shelves. "Ssso many." He turned to Ricky. "Thissss is power, real power."

Jibbawk stopped at a shelf, read the binding of a thick book and tapped his claws on it. "Who is this Harry Potter person?"

"Uh, that's fiction. Half of these books are not true. They're stories made up."

"What value is a fake ssstory?" Jibbawk raked the binding of the book with his claw. The book fell from the shelf.

"It's like a play. People love to read fake stories. Humans grow up and have to go to school. We learn facts all the time. It's nice to read something totally different and fun and not have to worry about the truth. Besides, fiction can be so exciting and out of this world. You can also learn from fiction. It has stuff in there based on reality, like emotions and drama and life lessons. You've told me an old fable about the Immortal Rulers. Fables are a form of fiction, too."

"That is not a fable, Earthling," Jibbawk snapped. "Though the stories cannot be confirmed, Shadics would not tell it if it weren't true."

"Sorry, I just didn't think immortality was possible." Ricky let Jibbawk walk ahead, clearly nervous he'd taken down Jibbawk's mood.

"Anything is posssible," Jibbawk hissed. "Lan Darr was one of the seven planets surveyed five hundred years ago by the Great Ones. It is possible my

planet holds the secret of immortality. The other worlds have long been conquered and thoroughly explored."

"Lucky you, to get Lan Darr." Ricky was trying to sound pleasing.

"No, not lucky. I've one of the ssstrongest bloodlines. Lan Darr is my blood right."

"How come it takes so long to conquer primitive worlds?"

Jibbawk stared at Ricky, trying to figure out if his question was an insinuation of weakness. "The Gods do not wish usss to move too fast. First, our explorers survey every valley, field, mountain and most ssspecies. We move tribes in one by one. Sssome die still, but most sssurvive. Then after proper integration, the war begins."

"Do you know what germs are?" Ricky said with a touch of amusement.

"Yesss, you have explained these invisible warriors to me," Jibbawk said suspiciously. "Because of your advanced knowledge, I'm willing to believe you."

"Yeah, sounds like you have to get used to the bacteria and viruses in a new world first. Otherwise, everyone would get sick and die."

Jibbawk and Ricky found the non-fiction section. Every time Jibbawk liked a book, he set it in a pile. At the end of the night, he sprinkled blue Hubbu pollen over the stacks, and they vanished, slipping through the folds of space, arriving somewhere on Lan Darr.

Jibbawk and Ricky traveled to new Libraries, bigger ones. Over time, the pair had collected over five-hundred-seventy-three textbooks.

But Jibbawk wanted more. He marveled over an introduction to the principals of flight but had a hard time finding specific books about how to build an airplane. There was some engineering math involving suspension bridges and skyscrapers. Jibbawk pointed to a picture of the Empire State Building. "I want one of those," he hissed.

"We're gonna have to go to a university library," Ricky said, finishing the breakfast cereal he'd retrieved the last trip and drinking down the powdered milk he said reminded him of home. Elinor sat next to him eating her cereal. It took Jibbawk a few weeks to get used to a female sitting at the table with men, but he allowed it to appease Earthling sensibilities. Ricky looked at her bowl, still half full, and dove his spoon in, stealing a bite. She slapped him, play-

fully.

Elinor closed the book she was reading. "I need a few more books when you go."

"Sure," Ricky said. "Give me a list."

She smiled and nodded. The two exchanged a long look between them.

Jibbawk was pleased with their connection, though he couldn't take too much of their nauseatingly gentle flirtation.

"It is time," he said and stood.

Ricky leaned to Elinor and whispered into her ear and joined Jibbawk in the middle of the great hall. Slaves handed them bags filled with water and snacks and more orange and blue Hubbu Pollen. Elinor handed Ricky a list of the books she wanted. More of the fiction kind.

"Why have we not gone to a universsity before?" Jibbawk asked.

"Uh, because they have security and bars on the windows and there are a lot of people around. It's going to be very hard to break into one."

Jibbawk took a pinch of orange pollen and held it over their heads. Ricky suggested, "I can go by myself. It would be easier to move and faster without having to hide you."

Jibbawk paused, considering the option. He did have a city to attend to. He knew the connection with Elinor would keep him in line. "Fine, you may go. You know what I desire. I've some factories to inspect today."

Jibbawk let Ricky go to Earth five more times by himself.

At the end of another month, the stacks included well over two thousand books. They were how-to's, college chemistry, algebra and geometry, manufacturing histories and economic theory books. Jibbawk even found an advanced farming book that will help increase food yields.

Round-the-clock teams organized and copied the texts. Jibbawk was keeping crucial weaponry designs to himself. His personal engineers played with trebuchets and fireworks and even constructed what Ricky called a potato gun.

Migration to Lan Darr tripled, everyone had jobs, and all companies were hiring. Finding talented and smart Shadics grew increasingly difficult because Jibbawk wasn't ready to advertise specific job requirements. He was afraid Cal-kaw or any of the other rulers would see his progress and come snooping around. If he were to have revenge on Cal-kaw

and his family, there could be no sharing of this new knowledge.

Ricky eventually branched out from obtaining books and turned his attention to supplies. He carefully stole tons of gear, tools, and necessities. He procured new clothes and even sent a letter to his parents and Elinor's. Jibbawk wasn't mad at this; he knew the boy would have to make contact with those whom he knew at some point.

During Ricky's last trip to Earth, he brought back a six-hundred-foot spool of copper wire, a huge crate of glass light bulbs and a box full of metal switches. However, he'd alerted security somehow.

Lupines

After sprinkling Hubbu on what he wanted, he was chased. Ricky barely had time to use the pollen on himself, right before a dog almost tore out his throat.

That did not please Jibbawk. He put a stop to his visits, temporarily, until he assessed his situation.

Chapter 10
Letting Go

Six months passed. Ricky hadn't been back to Earth, but he asked to go often. Jibbawk didn't say, but he wasn't really interested in sending Ricky back home ever again. Ricky was smart and had to explain lots of things to the Lan Darrians and Shadics. Plus, Jibbawk let an entire community of Lupines migrate and though they were very smart tinkerers, they needed lots of language instruction to catch up. Lupines were considered prize subjects by all Shadic rulers. They were small furry creatures with ten-foot-long tails and extended snouts, but their brains absorbed information at incredible speeds and they were easy to control.

Ricky and his female, Elinor, had become increasingly affectionate. Jibbawk often found them sitting very close to each other and even touching hands. It was good; they would be together forever whether they wanted to or not.

Jibbawk and Ricky still had their training sessions, but now many others were involved. Hundreds of Shadics, Lan Darrians and Lupines sat in training.

Storms, one right after the other, came from the East and filled up Dantia's parched canals. It was the beginning of the rainy season, which was a good season, a fruitful one. The overflow would flood the fields, and feed marshid and cedid invertebrates—which were delicacies to Shadics. The greater the floods, the larger the bloom of marshids. The creatures would inadvertently fertilize the fields as well. Dantians had much to celebrate.

Jibbawk, Ricky, Elinor, Halawk and over a hundred elders, military leaders and the smartest Shadics packed the great hall. Tables were brought in, as were extra slaves and Lan Darrian cooks. It was a celebration dinner. The Shadics had completed the first coal power plant. The party ate under five dangling, flickering lightbulbs. The plant was a small unit built on the roof. Coal fire heated the air sending it up a flue, turning a turbine. The turbine was connected to a coil of copper wire and created electricity, sending power through the capital building in wires stapled to the ceilings. Every hallway was now lit by light bulbs

as was the great dining hall. It was proof of concept. Two more coal power plants were being built near the wealthiest of the Shadic towers.

Lan Darr couldn't produce copper wire yet, but that was not any concern. When they needed more, they'd simply steal it from Earth.

The celebration went late, but eventually, the room cleared out. Those too drunk to leave found a quiet corner and slept.

After the dinner had ended, Ricky approached Jibbawk. "Sir, I was wondering if we could speak, alone."

Jibbawk nodded and motioned Ricky to follow him. He led the Earthling to the fireroom on the second floor. It was huge with plush chairs, an enormous fireplace and Shadic art along the walls. Jibbawk accepted a spicy drink from a slave. He cleared the room and took a seat near the fire. "Sssit. What is on your mind?"

Ricky sat. "I was wondering if you could send Elinor home. She's been so great. She really wants to see her family, show them she's okay. You promised to do so when we were done stealing the books."

Jibbawk thought for a moment. There was a nice routine in place, and he naively thought the humans might not desire to go home anymore. "You have ssserved me well, and she has behaved." He thought some more and sipped his drink. "But I simply cannot allow it. You will miss her. It will affect your work here."

"Seeing her upset and missing her family is affecting my work," Ricky said, his jaw set tight, and his face flushed red. "She'll come back, she promises."

Jibbawk sat up. "You musssst forget about Earth. You are a sslave to my rule and sso is she. If she is bored, I can add work to her daily life ssso that her hands are made more usseful and her mind will not wander as much."

Ricky leaned back, folding his arms tight across his chest. "I know you have slavery here, but you've never called me one."

"We have all been sslaves. We believe that it is our duty. Not one Shadic ssslave complains. It is your time now."

"You were a slave?" Ricky asked.

"Yes. All Shadics are born into ssslavery. We grow up in ssservitude, train while we work and when we are old enough, we are Tesssted. If we passs, we are releasssed into sssocciety. If we do not, we either die or remain ssslaves. The weak ones do not deserve

freedom, and they know it. This is how our culture became so strong. Everyone knows how important it is to begin as a slave."

"The more technologically advanced you get, the more you'll realize that slavery is wrong." Ricky stood and moved to the door.

"Sssit."

Ricky stopped. For a moment, Jibbawk thought he'd resist the order and force Jibbawk to sink a quill into his flesh. He returned to his seat slowly and without looking up.

"In purssuit of good, all men sssuffer," Jibbawk said, quoting a Shadic proverb over five thousand years old. He let that sink into Ricky's brain. "We have nothing but what we owe those that came before usss. Do you think you'd have the machines you have on Earth without the men that lived and died prior to your birth? The clothes? The cccities? The food on your table? You are indebted to them. I would not have control over Lan Darr if my raccce hadn't become ssso intelligent and powerful. I owe everything I do to the others that came before me. Ssso it was my duty, my honor, to ssserve our sssociety and our great families. You're a so-called genius, so you must understand the value of what I say."

"Will I ever be free?"

Jibbawk sipped his tea and stared into the fire. "No. You are different."

"You owe me and my people for the technology you are using. Maybe I'll just stop working for you. I'll protest." Anger filled the boy's eyes, too much anger.

Ricky needed to learn his place, quickly.

Jibbawk smiled and cleaned a couple of quills with his beak. After a considerable silence, he said, "Guards!" Two guards burst into the fire room. Ricky jumped to his feet. The shadics grabbed Ricky's arms and held him tight. Ricky kicked and thrashed but the more he moved, the tighter the guards gripped him. Finally, out of breath, he stopped kicking. Jibbawk strode up to him, plucking a long quill from his forearm. He leaned close to Ricky, staring at his watery, quivering eyes. "You have let your mouth become too loose, Earthling. Here is your consequence." Jibbawk touched the quill to Rickys' cheek.

"No no no!" Ricky shrieked.

Jibbawk pressed the quill into Ricky's skin, pushed it past his teeth and sunk it deep into his tongue. Ricky screamed as his body went into spasms. Jibbawk counted two seconds then pulled the quill.

Ricky fell and curled into a ball.

"Arressst this creature from Earth." Jibbawk spun and returned to his seat.

The guards grabbed Ricky's wrists and dragged him away.

Anderson Atlas

Chapter 11
A Conspiracy of Fire

Alarm bells woke Jibbawk from a deep sleep. He leaped out of his sleeping alcove, his quills standing on end. Jibbawk looked at the sundial drawn on the far wall. If it was daytime, the light would have shown through a tiny hole in the roof and pointed to a number carved into the wall. There was no light, meaning it was still night.

A guard flung open the door to his chamber. "Sir, the capital building is being attacked."

"What?" Jibbawk snapped. "Who's is it?"

"They are not Shadics. They are Lan Darrians."

Jibbawk hissed. "Insolence."

Jibbawk threw his cloak over his shoulders, yanked on his alanx-bindings and his helmet-crown and stomped to the stairs as fast as he could while maintaining his composure. He looked through a small window at the bottom of the winding steps. A massive crowd surrounded the capital building. The crowd was mostly seated, holding hands and chanting. Some held lanterns, but not a weapon could be seen. There must have been ten thousand. The island the capital building sat on was packed, shoulder to shoulder and the canal across the way was full of protestors as well. Light rain drenched the crowd, but they didn't seem to care.

They weren't actually attacking the capital. This was weird to Jibbawk. Revolts were always bloody battles. Never before had a protest been non-violent. Jibbawk smirked. *How foolish they are.* One of Ricky's books mentioned this type of tactic, but Jibbawk had ignored it, believing it to be proof of the ridiculous weakness of Earthling empires.

Violent or not, any protest is an attack. There was no other way to deal with insistent populations. He had to destroy their notions of control and fast. They needed to know who the father of this world was and will always be.

Jibbawk marched to the front door, waited for the Shadic slaves to pull them open and then strode to the edge of the steps. "What is the meaning of his?" he yelled to the crowd.

A large Lan Darrian stood and stepped forward. He was one of the coal miners evidenced by his leather shirt, pants, cuffs, and gloves. His scales were black and as smooth as glass, and his eyes were

a piercing blue. "You're robbing us to the point of starvation! You've increased taxes three hundred percent." Six other Lan Darians stepped up. Jibbawk didn't see them as people with humble desires or unmet needs. He saw them as simple stones, waiting to be knocked over.

A handful of Lupines came up and stopped next to the Lan Darrians. "We don't like your new taxes, ruler Jibbawk. We came to Lan Darr without any tax on us at all. This benefited your new city, greatly. When you added the consumption tax, we did not protest. But when you added a working tax of over fifty percent, we cannot help but speak up." The little Lupine had a big voice for his size.

The Lan Darrian who had spoken before added, "Return the taxes to pre-third quarter levels, or we will do nothing at all. We will strike!" The crowd roared in unison.

Jibbawk plucked a quill so fast, no one noticed. He stepped down the first stair and flung it. It pierced the forehead of the tall Lan Darrian. "I am your ruler! You do as I say and without question!"

The Lan Darrian fell back, spasming. Someone pulled the quill. The crowd continued to chant louder than before.

Jibbawk flung quill after quill into the crowd. The capital building housed a dozen Shadics, and they were following Jibbawk down the marble steps, flinging poison darts as fast as they could.

The protestors erupted into chaos, scrambling to escape the small island the capital was on, but the two bridges were narrow. Many leaped into the canal to escape. Jibbawk tried to nail a swimming Lupine, but the water slowed the quill to an ineffective speed. Jibbawk roared with frustration.

The twenty-two surrounding towers housed a population of over a thousand Shadics. The slaves, the soldiers, the workers, the owners of businesses all came out of their houses. Even though they were outnumbered twenty to one, they had enormous strength. They threw quill after quill into the crowd from their side of the canal. The protestors were trapped. The soldier Shadics also had cudgels, some preferred swords. They lashed out at any Lan Darrian or Lupine without mercy. Jibbawk was handed his scepter. He found a writhing citizen and bashed in his head until he went still.

When it was over, bodies covered the grounds around the capital building and the surrounding streets. It poured rain and Jibbawk let the water wash

the blood and brain from his scepter. He returned to his building without hesitation or regret.

He spoke to a guard at the door before it was closed. "Throw the bodies into boats and parade them around the cccity for two days. Let them smell the stink of their dead. Shut down any funerals, by forccce if necessary, and do not let them put up tomb-stones or markers. Arrest the ones that have been dosed with poison, but have not died. They will dig in the mines without pay or breaks for six months." Jibbawk returned to his bed alcove and slept like a hatchling.

Deep winter set into Dantia. The chill frosted the stones of its buildings and made chunks in the salty canal waters. Then, as though the cold wasn't enough, Dantia was hit with the worst snowstorm it had seen in over a hundred years.

Two thousand Shadics died in their beds; the Lan Darrian and Lupine deaths were not counted, but it wasn't nearly that many.

Jibbawk covered himself in reams of woolen coats from yats and ventured out into the cold. He had to do something. It wasn't cold enough to be killing Shadics. They were too strong, too warm in their blood. Something was amiss.

He'd visited the homes of the dead. They were as they always were, save for the coal they burned instead of wood. But according to Ricky's books, there was little difference between burning coal or wood, only coal lasted longer and stored better. Jibbawk didn't know what to do. He'd gone ten years on Lan Darr and not had this many deaths. Jibbawk crossed the frozen grass around the capital building and boarded his boat. Ice filled the canal waters, but only in chunks. His rowers pushed through it, smashing up the larger chunks with iron bars.

The boat headed down the main canal to the outskirts of Dantia. One of the tallest buildings in town was there, built into the side of the massive wall. It had thin slits for windows and was over ten stories tall. Stairs on the outside wound around the tower. Inside were prison cells. The building's stone was drab and dull, and its doorways were iron reinforced.

Jibbawk hiked to the top floor. A guard on the inside opened, and Jibbawk entered, He shed the snow-dusted coats and handed them to the guard. The stink was irritating. Cries and yells echoed

through the walls.

Jibbawk walked to the end of the hall and opened the steel-plated door. It was dingy and dark inside, about ten by twenty feet. Ricky slept in the corner, huddled in a ball. Jibbawk could see that he'd taken off his clothes and crammed them in the window to try to keep out the chill.

Jibbawk kicked the boy with his massive, clawed foot. "Creature from Earth, get up."

Ricky opened his eyes, looked at Jibbawk then closed them again.

Jibbawk grabbed Ricky's arm and pulled him off the floor. He held a quill to his throat. "I can end your meager life if you wish. It will be the mossst painful exit."

"What do you want with me?" Ricky was very thin and covered in mud and soot.

"You are a genius, are you not? I will be willing to reduccce your ssssentenccce if you help me."

"Get me out of here!" Ricky screamed. "I want to see Elinor!" Ricky spat. He shivered violently.

Jibbawk pulled him close. "Then you will be a loyal ssservant and expect nothing more. Am I undersssstood?"

"Yes, yes, anything you wish."

Jibbawk waited for Ricky to dress in his dingy clothes, pushed Ricky out of the cell and down the hall to the exit. He put on his coats and gave one to Ricky. Ricky only made it down a few steps before his legs gave out. He fell and rolled to a landing. Jibbawk picked up the creature from Earth and put him under his arm, carrying him down the rest of the way to the boat.

Snow fell from the solid gray clouds and the wind howled. The oarsmen rowed the boat down the icy canal toward the capital building.

"I need water," Ricky mumbled through his fierce shivering. Jibbawk scooped some water from the canal and gave it to him. Ricky drank even though people dumped their waste into it.

At the capital, Ricky was given clothes and sat next to the fire. Elinor was brought up from the basement where she was sewing. She called Ricky's name and fell to him. She cradled him in her arms and cried.

After a few minutes, Jibbawk had enough. "Okay, enough of your sentimental blubbering," he said. "Ricky, why are people dying in their homes? This is the first winter we've been burning coal for heat and the first winter we've had so many deathsss.

Can it be from the coal?"

Ricky investigated one of the newer heaters. It was a round metal pan with a narrow top venting pipe made of steel and tin. After some consideration, the boy had an idea. "I think there isn't enough air getting to the coals, so they're creating carbon monoxide instead of carbon dioxide. That would poison people. It would be the same if you burned wood in this device." Ricky explained that the lid needed to be taller with larger vent holes. "Fixing this wouldn't affect its efficiency at all, I'm not sure why the lid was made so small."

"A Lupine company made these. They are fancy and only sold to Shadics." Jibbawk stomped. "They have done this on purpose!" he kicked over one of the chairs.

"No! I don't think they intended this," Ricky replied. "Anyone could make this mistake. Earthlings die from carbon monoxide poisoning all the time. That's why we learned about it in school."

Jibbawk relaxed, keeping his suspicion hidden inside, for now.

Over the next month, Ricky helped Jibbawk and a handful of Lupines and Shadic engineers refit the fancy new heaters with proper air holes, metal shells and vents.

Ricky fell back into old habits with Jibbawk, holding his tongue tighter to his lips in more respect-ful ways. Classes with Ricky resumed. Two more power plants opened, making four altogether and a larger, stronger bridge now spanned the widest part of the river delta.

Although there were still rebel meetings and secret groups, Jibbawk's guard easily sniffed them out. As long as there were regular, public killings, the people of Dantia seemed to fall in line.

Chapter 12
The Unexpected Comes Fast

The spring switch finally arrived. On Lan Darr, a strange thing happens to winter. A few days of torrential, hot rain from the south, melts the snow pack, fills the rivers and warms the air. Winter is gone within a day. All the storms and wind that come from the south are fierce but welcome.

During the harsh winter, Jibbawk allowed some measure of laziness. He slept a lot and ventured out very little. Food stores ran out early and eventually hunger set in. But Pyramid buds filled the valleys promising great blooms, the well grass was practically bursting out of the mud and great boggie fruits filled with the rain like water balloons.

The survivors of the winter got back to work, but progress was slow. Jibbawk became frustrated with the pace of research and development. It seemed like the Lan Darrians weren't working as efficiently as they had before the crackdown on protestors. Jibbawk and his soldiers still had to kill someone almost every day. The public square was full of rotting corpses stuffed on spikes, so much so, everyone avoided the area. The buildings around the square emptied out as Lan Darrian's preferred a tent on the outskirts than a real home near the stench.

The Lupine engineers ran into more and more problems, and Jibbawk suspected they were intentionally sabotaging progress.

More Shadic immigration came from across the galaxy, and as fast as an apartment or home was left vacant by death or imprisonment, they were filled with a Shadic family.

The third day of the three moon cycle had been a gloriously warm day. No one had to be killed (yet), and everyone showed up to the mines and factories. The fourth power plant fired up that morning and powered three additional Shadic towers and two production facilities.

Jibbawk was in a particularly good mood. If this continued, he'd lift the curfew and maybe lower the taxes a little. He was lounging on the rooftop with his favorite female, Jib-Selawk, eating and drinking and becoming intoxicated. He'd insisted Ricky and

Elinor join him.

"Drink up," Jibbawk said, ordering a slave to fill the Earthling's cups. "Today is a good day. You're Earth technology is changing all of usss for the better." Jibbawk walked Ricky to the railing and pointed. "Sssee your lights. Be proud." The three Shadic towers glowed brighter from their windows than from the oil lamp-lit ones. Jibbawk could see pride in Ricky's smile.

Ricky gulped his drink and coughed on the strong flavor. After his second round, he began swaying in the stiff wind and so did Elinor, though they were all smiles.

Jibbawk's slave handed Ricky and Elinor two more drinks.

Jibbawk raised his hand, spilling accidentally. "Dantia was frail and on the edge of destruction, but lately, she's beginning to awaken."

Jib-Selawk stumbled up to him and took the goblet from his claws. She gave him a narrow look and swallowed it down. "Dantians have learned how lenient or brutal you can be. They are beginning to choose the easier of the two pathways because you made it clear there are only two choices," the female Shadic said. Jibbawk turned to her and eyed her carefully, but playfully. She pecked Jibbawk in the chest where his quills were the shortest. He recoiled but was smiling at the edge of his beak. Jibbawk's slave had a new drink in his hand within seconds.

"Countlesss uprisings have plagued the Shadic Empire, but none ssset in ssso quickly as this. Usually it takesss more than ten years to sssee insssurgents build into a movement."

"It's your taxes," Ricky said, slurring his speech. "There just a bit much. They'll have a tea party soon and it will be fantastic." He and Elinor chuckled. The wind toyed with his hair, which had grown past his shoulders. The two attempted to hold each other up. They whispered to each other and laughed. Elinor kissed Ricky's cheek then laid her head on his shoulder. This pleased Jibbawk. He'd never seen them kiss. Besides Ricky's contribution, Elinor was a talented seamstress. Her stitching was turning heads all over Dantia and creating a fashion trend that helped quell some of the negativity. Jibbawk was eager to put her to work, creating a new wardrobe for his government.

"It's not only the taxes. It's also because you're a Nazi," Elinor mumbled. She smiled tipped her head to the side, then spun back into Rickys'

arms, laughing.

Jibbawk didn't know or care what a Nazi was. He waved a slave over. "Bring in the wompans! I want music tonight." A minute later there were two drummers, a kootie player, and a singer. The drummer beat a lively and energetic rhythm, and the kootie sewed an enchanting melody.

Jibbawk told the servant to give Ricky and Elinor more drinks.

"I can't," Ricky said.

"Me either," Elinor chimed, finding stability less and less possible. It made Jibbawk laugh.

"One more drink and then you can go to bed," Jibbawk ordered. The slave filled their cups. He watched them down the strong alcohol. They both held on to each other and the railing and swayed to the music. Jibbawk laughed. They were being silly and gazing into each other's eyes.

"Now I will dance!" Jibbawk and Jib-Selawk danced around each other. His shoulders moved up and down with the rhythm. The two turned together, touched chests then moved apart. Jibbawk pushed her shoulder teasingly, and she fell to the floor. The female pecked at his leg then stood and hugged him. They did this semi-violent dance, ignoring Ricky and

Elinor's stares. Their quills were standing straight out.

Elinor turned. "I've to go. I'm going to be sick."

Jibbawk waved her away.

Elinor lost her grip on Ricky and fell back. Ricky tried to catch her but his foot twisted and he fell the opposite way, hitting his head on the railing. Elinor rolled to her stomach and threw up all over the floor.

The music didn't stop, and neither did Jibbawk. He pushed Jib-Selawk again, staring at her beautiful, bright orange eyes. Her clawed foot stepped on the vomit and slipped, throwing the shadic female backward. She put her arm back to catch herself, but there was Elinor. Her Flalanx quills stabbed Elinor's back, and a dozen back quills pierced Elinor's neck and arm. She screamed.

Ricky jumped up, his eyes wide. "NO!"

Jib-Selawk rolled off Elinor, trailing blood in fat droplets. The music stopped. Ricky pulled Elinor to his lap and shook her. "Hey, come on, wake up." She wasn't moving, and her eyes had rolled into the back of her head.

Jibbawk picked up Jib-Selawk and threw her across the rooftop. "Look what you've done!"

Ricky rolled Elinor over. The punctures were

deep and bleeding heavily. He checked her pulse. He checked her chest. He shook her again.

Elinor had stopped breathing, and foam spilled from her agape mouth.

Ricky became irate. He screamed and yelled incoherently at Jib-Selawk. He cried and buried his head in Elinor's chest. He leaned away and vomited then kissed her cold cheek.

Jib-Selawk rolled her eyes and sat back on the lounger. "She should not have been under me."

A large black carrion bird landed on the railing to carry her soul to Otisius. The bird eyed Elinor's body. Normally, Jibbawk would let it feast on her flesh as a way to appease the gods, but he knew enough about Earth customs not to allow it. He shooed the bird away.

"Take her body to the basement and call a doctor," Jibbawk ordered, though he knew there wasn't much to do. Shadic poison could not be remedied. Ricky's tears flowed. He held onto her hand as she was carried away.

Anger filled Jibbawk. He had just won back Ricky's loyalty. How would he ever regain it? Jibbawk pulled Jib-Selawk close to him. She smiled, thinking they would return to their mating dance. Instead, Jibbawk snapped her neck.

After tossing Jib-Selawk off the roof, Jibbawk marched to his ruling chamber, slamming the door shut behind him.

Halawk looked up from an Earth book. "Something has happened," he said.

Jibbawk swayed on his feet. "Nothing I can't handle."

The door to the room flew open. It was a Shadic guard. "Ruler, we have a problem."

Jibbawk wasn't in the mood to handle any more issues. He was moments from going on a killing spree, just to make himself feel better. "Out with it."

"The boy from Earth is gone. I locked him and the dead girl in the basement. When the doctor came, I took him to her body to see if there was anything that could be done. She was there, Ricky was . . . gone."

Jibbawk leaped at the guard and seized his throat. "You locked the door, didn't you?"

"Always sir, both locks were engaged," the guard squeezed out of his compressed larynx.

"You will lock this building down and search every floor until you find him. Surround the grounds

as well. He can't have gone far." Fighting every nerve, Jibbawk released his grip.

"Yes, ruler," the guard croaked.

The night was a long one. Jibbawk and a dozen guards searched the building and around it, but Ricky was gone. They moved street to street but had no luck. Every Shadic that was awoken threw aside the confines of sleep and isolation and joined the hunt. The boy must have been as fast as a Kiet.

Jibbawk stood at Dantia's massive gates. Their height towered over him and blocked out the three sliver moons. The gate spanned the wide canal but also had plenty of walking space on either side. It was the only way in or out of Dantia, at least for a weak human.

A dark feeling came over Jibbawk. Though it wasn't his fault Jib-Selawk landed on the Earth girl; he knew it was the worst thing that could have happened.

Chapter 13
Not Fast Enough

Jibbawk didn't sleep for weeks. He had too much to do. He continued collecting taxes, trade was controlled, and travel monitored. The spy division rooted out the ever-increasing rebel groups and criminals were hung without trial.

A month passed, and Jibbawk found himself standing on the grass in front of his tall capital building. At the edge of the grass were a dozen hanging Lan Darrians who had been convicted of sneaking around Dantia after dark. It wasn't a great offense, but every broken rule would lead to another one if not treated seriously. Jibbawk would regain control at any cost. The bodies were bloating and rotting, but he'd decided to keep them there for now because the city center was already full of the dead and decaying. The fear of death used to work to keep subordinates in line, but its overwhelming effect was wearing off. People simply averted their eyes and kept away.

Halawk strode up to Jibbawk and handed him a box of tax receipts. It was mostly empty. "Revenue

has fallen again. It is now far below what it was when we started raising them." His wise eyes were suggesting lowering them, but Jibbawk wouldn't hear it. "They don't have any more gold to plunder."

"The Lan Darrian's will break. Then, and only then, will we remove the high taxes." Jibbawk stared at the lifeless body, hanging in front of him. "Meanwhile, find a hundred more able males and put them to work in the gold mines. I've an empire to build."

"You will not have an empire left if this keeps going on," Halawk said wisely. "But you are the ruler, and I will do as you wish." Halawk walked back toward the capital.

Jibbawk yelled after him, "I will commission a new capital building. One that is twicccce as tall!" Jibbawk's voice was harsh and strained. "Lan Darr will be the most powerful empire in all of the system! I will become one of the Immortal Rulers. I've never known anything so strongly."

He paced back and forth while the sky darkened with thick storm clouds. He found a spot in between the hanging corpses and sat cross-legged, meditating until his heart rate was a more manageable pounding.

Lan Darrian slaves pulled up in a carrier boat

and tied it to the capital dock. They unloaded half a dozen boxes of marshids and fried oap skins for the feast. Jibbawk moved to follow them, his stomach empty and wanting, but was stopped by a group of Shadic slaves holding a much larger crate between them. One of Jibbawk's generals followed them, his eyes wide and gleaming. "Ruler, I have a gift. The first of many from the smelter, Towest, at the south river. They are very successful in casting metals."

The slaves set the crate down and popped the top. Inside were a dozen rifles. They were crudely cast, had rough edges where the halves met, and the metal was discolored, but they were beautiful. "I've tested them myself and they are very powerful indeed."

Jibbawk took a long rifle out of the box and inspected it. "Are your spies still in place on Cicanth?" Jibbawk asked the general.

He nodded. "They are watching Cal-kaw as we speak."

"So he does not know of our ability to produce the rifles?"

"No. However, he knows of the electricity." The general took a bag of gun powder from the box.

"I suppose that could not be avoided." Jib-

bawk aimed the rifle.

"I'm sure you've heard, but he does plan on visiting Dantia himself. He's very much interested in trading secrets."

"I'm sure he is. Now show me how to fire this thing."

The general showed Jibbawk how to load and fire it. He poured powder into the end and dumped in the shot pellets and added the primer to the hammer. He took one knee, aimed at one of the hanging bodies and fired. The boom startled the slaves toting in the food. The bloated body exploded, gushing puss and rot.

The power of the rifle impressed Jibbawk. He reloaded and fired again and again and again. The pain in his shoulder made him smile.

"Good. Take these and distribute and train every guard stationed in my capital building. Then make me a thousand of these by the end of the month," Jibbawk ordered.

A month would never pass.

That night, Jibbawk sat at the head of the long dining table, staring at a full load of food. The huge table was surrounded with elder Shadics and his army generals; fifty others total. The feast was to commemorate the first of the spring harvests.

Jibbawk started with the grilled meek bats and ate some berries. A Shadic slave refilled his tall goblet.

Halawk filled his mouth with the fresh marshids- the ones just brought in. "Someone is illegally importing goods from Ceevis," he said with a mouth full. "We found another stash in the forest today. It is hard to control the trade, almost not worth it."

Jibbawk finished his drink in one gulp. "We cannot have illegal trade. The ancientss have sssaid that during these revoltsss the population mussst look to usss to be the sssaviors. We will oppressss them but always show them hope. It is a delicate balanccce. If they trade with others they will look to others for solutions. I need them to need me. I'm the father of Lan Darr."

The rest of the table banged their goblets in approval of his statement.

Halawk nodded and swallowed his mouthful. "Yes, but they already know that the trade can relieve their desperation, even momentarily. It is one thing for your subjects to believe you will stop the punishment, and quite another to feel like it will nev-

er end. For if it never ends they will have no choice but to throw off the government that binds them."

"What are you ssssaying?" Jibbawk stabbed a piece of marshid and brought it near his mouth. "That I should give in? Show mercy? Will this not show weaknesss in my rule? Will thisss not strip every ounce of power I have built?" Jibbawk's anger rose from his bowels and ran out every quill on his body.

Halawk choked on his marshid tentacle. He spat and spat until his mouth was clear of the food, but still choked. Foam came from his throat, filled his mouth and spilled out of his clipped beak. He pushed back from the table and stood, gripping his neck. His eyes were wild, and his pupils fixed on Jibbawk.

Jibbawk looked at Halawk's plate. He'd only touched the marshid tentacles. Jibbawk eyed the tentacle stabbed on his fork and then threw it across the room. One of his great generals choked and fell back. Then another. Five more died in only a few moments. The others stood and backed away from the food.

Jibbawk stormed into the slave room, but there were only Shadics in there. He looked at the crate brought in by the Lan Darrians, touching a marshid with his claw. It seemed to have a slimy coating on it. The slaves backed away from him, silent eyes wild. Jibbawk kicked the crate so hard it slid across the floor and smashed to pieces on the wall.

He threw off his royal cloak, his helmet and his Alanx-cuffs and his quills stood on end. "So the battle begins," he mumbled. "Guards, subjects, generals! Round up my entire army. Tonight, they die!" Jibbawk ran to a window and looked out. He could see torches light up one by one until the alleys and canals and walkways were filled. The citizens revolt was well at hand. "Someone bring me one of the guns."

The Shadics who lived around the capital building will come out to fight at any moment. Jibbawk had protocols for this. Blood would run through the streets, and he would drink it with pleasure.

Meanwhile, every resident of the capital building came down into the great hall, ready to fight. There were over a hundred loyal Shadics. Even the dozens of Shadic slaves would fight for Jibbawk.

Jibbawk took a rifle and loaded it. He pointed the muzzle out of the window and waited. The attackers would have to cross the canal first, and that would make them easy targets. Jibbawk was flanked

by a dozen armed guards; all pointing rifles out of the windows. He wished he had a gun for every guard, but what they had will do.

"Fire into the crowd and don't sssstop," Jibbawk ordered. He aimed and fired. The crack of the guns echoed around the great hall like explosive pinging balls. The end result could not be seen in the dark, but it didn't matter. Jibbawk loaded up and fired again. So did all his guards.

The city alarm bells on top of the Shadic towers rang and rang. Jibbawk stopped firing and stared at the crowd. They didn't dare try to cross the two bridges to the capital building, but they weren't dispersing. They were singing a filthy, disgusting song.

> *We will be free,*
> *Form the pinnacle to the sea,*
> *We will be judged by the same laws*
> *That Shadics ignore so easily.*
> *Ricky has shown us the way,*
> *His books have saved our day.*
> *We will have Life, Freedom, and Liberty!*

Jibbawk scowled. Where was his army? They should have started beating back the rebels. He paced, finally turning to one of the generals. "Where is your fourth regiment? Why have they not reported to us by now?"

The general watched out one of the windows. "I do not know. We have very strict plans to adhere to. If they are not kept, it can only be because the fourth regiment has been destroyed."

Jibbawk roared and grabbed the first thing he could, which was a wooden, intricately carved chair. He threw it at the general. The chair smashed into the general's back and broke into pieces. Jibbawk roared. "Go into the crowd and find your soldiers. You cannot come back without them." He pushed the general towards the door.

"It's the food, ruler Jibbawk. The marshids were delivered this evening, a fresh catch. They must have been poisoned. All our soldiers received a portion of the catch for tonight's feast," the general stated while standing up straight. Jibbawk scowled. The general understood the scowl and bowed. "I will return with definitive word on the state of your army, ruler, or I will not return at all."

The general motioned for two slaves to open the door, but he didn't get a chance to leave. As he stood waiting, he was shot in the head.

Jibbawk spun toward the stairway at the back

of the great hall. There was the boy from Earth. He was holding a long rifle and dressed in the uniform of an Ophex soldier.

Jibbawk's quills stood on end, doubling his apparent size.

Ricky licked his thumb, flicked it across the sight of his rifle, aimed and fired. The general closest to the stairs lost half of his skull and dropped like a sack of sludge.

"I'd rather have had the US infantry with me, but couldn't find the orange pollen. So I brought some other friends," Ricky called out.

From higher up the stairs came a roar. They were all Ophex soldiers, wearing the same dull gray outfits and odd round helmets. All were armed with guns. They surrounded Ricky and fired.

Jibbawk hissed. He threw his arms out to either side and ran toward Ricky. Ricky lifted his rifle up again. Jibbawk's generals fired back at the stairs and immediately reloaded.

The Ophex guns reloaded automatically giving them an upper hand.

Their guns fired. A dozen generals went down as they struggled to pour powder into thier barrels.

Jibbawk flipped in the air and was not hit.

He had jumped so far and so high it took Ricky by surprise. He landed, lunged and seized Ricky by the throat. "How did you get in here?" Jibbawk mumbled.

Five shock poles were thrust into Jibbawk's sides, ribs and neck. Electricity bit into the Shadic ruler, and he released Ricky and fell.

Ricky rubbed his throat. "All the time you kept me, and Elinor locked up in the basement we dug ourselves a little tunnel. I knew one day I'd need it. Never thought I'd have to break in through it, but hey, it's all cool daddy-o."

An Ophex pointed his rifle at Jibbawk and shot him in the chest. Jibbawk blacked out, the pain a welcome reprieve to his absolute failure.

Chapter 14
He Who is Immortal, Gets the Last Laugh

Jibbawk awoke in the basement of his own capitol building. He was underneath a pile of dead Shadic generals and slaves. The blood that pooled on the bricks had dried to a dark black. Quills from the dead shadics stabbed him in uncomfortable places, and his nose was assaulted by the stench. He pushed off the bodies and stood. Pain shot through his nerves. He looked at his chest. Sure enough, he had been shot. Jibbawk fell to his butt. He laid back on the dead and waited for a moment.

A fat, furry ipcat came up to him, sniffing his quills, seeing if it could eat Jibbawk. He sat up, slowly this time. The ipcat scurried off. Jibbawk inspected his wound. There wasn't a lot of blood, and though the chest was a vulnerable area, Shadics had a large amount of fatty tissue around the muscle core of their backbones. His vital organs were on either side of the fatty space and were unhurt. He shut off the

pain and got to his feet. This wasn't over yet.

He marched up the short stairway to the door and banged on it. "Open thisss door. You've no right to keep me here. I am the father of Lan Darr!" he screamed so loud his voice cracked. He clutched his chest with one hand, applying pressure so the bleeding wouldn't increase.

Smoke assaulted his nostrils. They were burning down his capitol building!

Jibbawk turned, plucked a quill and threw it at the ipcat. It hit the small creature, killing it instantly.

Jibbawk shuffled to the dead thing and stabbed it with a sharp claw. He pulled its head off, ate it and then stripped the creatures furry skin off. Blood dripped down his beak and onto his quills, but this was no time for cleanliness.

Jibbawk quickly ate the guts and meat, knowing he'd need the energy it would provide. It tasted foul like rotten fish, but its taste didn't matter. He sucked the meat off the longest rib and one of the back thighs.

Jibbawk returned to the door. It wasn't barricaded, only held fast by a simple metal latch.

He carefully stuck the two bones through the crack in the door. The thighbone tripped the trigger, and then he lifted the latch with the rib. The door swung open, its hinges creaking loudly in the silent building.

Smoke filled the stairwell, Jibbawk sucked in a deep breath and ran. He jumped over flames and through billowing, dark clouds of ash and soot.

The tapestry gifts he had been given by the local Lan Darrians were in flames; the great wood table entirely engulfed as were all the chairs. Jibbawk made his way to the third floor. He found one of the bigger windows and, without looking, jumped out.

The grassy area around the building was muddied by water. They'd soaked the ground to prevent the fire from spreading. Jibbawk kicked at the puddle. Rage filled him to the top of his crown. He could see across one of the canals, but the streets were empty. Jibbawk crept along the building to the front and peeked around the corner.

There was a crowd filling the street across from the front of the capital building. Ricky, one of the Lan Darrians and a tall Ophex leader, stood with their backs to the flames.

The Ophex removed his helmet and brought a cone up to his mouth. It amplified his voice. Jibbawk could hear him even though he was over two hun-

dred yards away. "I hereby proclaim Lan Darr, FREE!" He said in English. So Ricky had been busy.

The crowd roared.

"Ophex offered over two thousand troops and many weapons to Lan Darr. We set up government to aid in rebuilding. As of now, do as you please without Shadic tyranny."

A young Lupine pointed at Jibbawk. "There's one!" The crowd erupted with shouting.

Jibbawk turned and ran, leaping over the canal and across worn pathways. He was so fast; he quickly outpaced any pursuers.

He left the city of Dantia behind. At the edge of the where the canal became the river, he bathed the dried blood off his body. The bullet hole in his chest hurt and would get infected if he didn't dress it. Jibbawk found the fabric-like bark of the lilp tree and made himself a bandage. He tied the bandage to his wound with a pliable vine.

Even if they hadn't followed him now, they would hunt him. He needed to find seclusion so he could heal.

Jibbawk hiked through the two-thousand-foot cliffs and across the vast plains. Anger filled his every nerve. He thought about his mistakes, his oversights. He thought about how the news of his defeat would reach his mother's ear holes. Cal-Kaw would rejoice, so would the Madd family. It was sickening. Even as a young peck, Jibbawk hadn't known failure. He was so quick and so smart. It wasn't an easy feeling to sit with. He was reminded of something his father had said. "Success is a sweet drop of blood and is fine to taste, but failure can lead to even greater feasts." There were lessons to learn and a way to still end up on top.

Finally, he arrived at the forest sinkholes. The holes were huge in the grasslands with sheer cliffs along the edges. Many of the larger ones were thousands of feet across and over a hundred feet deep. Below were rainforest microclimates. Plants and trees filled every available space.

Jibbawk spent the next day collecting vines and tying them together. When he had a long enough rope, he lowered himself down the rocky cliff side to the bottom. It took him over two hours of careful descent, but he made it.

A huge cavern tunnel was at the bottom of the cliff, with jagged rocks along the bottom, the top full of stalactites and thin crystals. It was twenty feet

high. Jibbawk headed into the enormous dark cave and a while later and ended up at another sink hole.

It turned out that all the holes were connected by small or large cavern tunnels. The network was miles and miles, but not one sinkhole could be climbed out of. The cliffs were too sheer and tall. Each sinkhole exposed to the sky was thick with trees, bushes, vines, spiny tacti.

Jibbawk smiled. No one would find him down here. The locals were afraid of the muggy, darkness and there were rumors of twelve-foot insiters and swarming, biting flips.

Jibbawk returned to the rope he'd used to enter the sinkhole. In the nearby cave, he made a bed out of huge, flat leaves and mud. He collected wood for a small fire and headed into the thick jungle to search for food.

After hours hunting in multiple jungle areas, Jibbawk noticed signs that he was not alone. No, there was someone else down here with him. The stench was familiar. Jibbawk searched the ground. Two cave systems away he stumbled upon a fire pit with smoldering coals. There was a hand print in the soil, too, a human hand print. *Strange.*

Jibbawk followed snapped twigs and scuff

marks on rocks for hundreds of yards. He entered one of the smaller caves while following the human's trail. When it ended, Jibbawk straightened up. The human must be close. Jibbawk noticed a space in the rocks to his left. Leaves and debris covered the hole. Jibbawk leaped onto the rocks, drove his hand down into the leaves and found the human. He grabbed flesh and hauled him out of his hiding spot.

The human was old and male. He had long gray hair and a beard that grew down to his stomach. He wore tattered and stained clothing similar to the style Ricky preferred.

"Please, don't hurt me, Jibbawk," the old man blubbered.

Jibbawk slammed the old man on the rocks and scratched his cheek just to see him bleed. "I feel like killing every human in the galaxy."

The old man held his hands up in a defensive position, but Jibbawk simply clawed at them, splitting the skin wide open. The old man cried out and cradled his hands.

"Please, please," is all he could say.

"What are you good for? You remind me of all that I hate." Jibbawk sat back on his feet. He contemplated the next wound he would inflict. "How long

have you been here?" Jibbawk asked. He reached over and clawed through the old man's shirt, cutting his shoulder. "And don't lie to me."

"I've been trapped here over a year, I think."

"Why did you come?"

"I . . . I've been to a dozen Hubbu worlds before I ended up here. I learned of a powerful insect and have been chasing it ever since."

"Earthlings don't know about Hubbu." Jibbawk's curiosity was thoroughly peaked.

"I hit a creature with my car a year ago. It had clothes like I've never seen and a really long tail.

"A Lupine."

"Yes. He was searching for the insect and told me all about it. It...it could give you everlasting life."

"The more you tell me, the more you get to live." Jibbawk's red eyes fixated on the old man.

"The Lupine died, but told me about Hubbu travel and gave me a lot of pollen. In exchange, I promised to continue the search, and when I found it, I'd deliver it to his brother on Ceevis." The old man wrapped some of his tattered jacket over the cuts on his hands. "I found it. Let me live, and I will show you what it looks like. There's plenty of the insects for you and me."

Jibbawk looked the man over. "If what you say is true, why are you not already immortal? You still bleed like everyone else."

The old man shook his head. "I am immortal, but I can still be cut!" he snapped. "I only need to find a way out of this cave. My rope was torn on a stone, and I cannot find another way up the sheer cliff."

"Show me this insect, and I will let you live out your immortality." Jibbawk stood. He no longer felt the pain in his wound or the failing of his pride. He was revisiting the old stories he'd heard as a child. The stories of the Immortal Rulers.

Young Shadics know the story by heart. It says that after the galaxy was conquered, the smartest, strongest ruler would be visited by the leader of the screp beetles. They would bring a sacrifice of a thousand screps. Each beetle would bite the ruler in turn. When they had delivered their poison, they'd die, but the Shadic ruler wouldn't. He would feel a new power in his muscles. He could jump higher, throw farther and out-think even his brightest enemies. The Shadic would never die and would become the first of the Infinite Rulers. There will only ever be five. Jibbawk had first heard this story when he was only eight years old but had instantly felt like he was des-

tined to meet the leader of the screps. The screps were said to be the only beetle in the galaxy that makes its own light along its shell.

As an adult, Jibbawk often fantasized about becoming an Infinite Ruler but didn't allow himself to become obsessed.

Now, things were becoming clear to Jibbawk. His destiny was unveiling itself.

Jibbawk followed the man through the forest for a long while. Eventually, they came to a pool of water. It was a dozen feet across, but very deep. The water was steaming hot, and crystal clear, looking like glass. Near the far side was a flat stone. The human carefully found his way to the stone and lifted it up.

"This is where I last saw one. It's the colorful one we need to find." There was nothing under the stone. He moved another one. Jibbawk helped lift stones as well. "It's a large black beetle. You'll know it when you find it."

As the sun started to set Jibbawk found one. It was a strange looking beetle unlike any he'd seen before. He grabbed it by its shell. It had eight legs and huge pinchers. It tried to pinch him, but couldn't bend its head back. It had ridges that ran down the upper thorax and the back shell. Little bioluminescent lights flickered down the ridges. The lights quickened as the beetle struggled.

The old man came to Jibbawk. "Oh, good. You found the right one. Some don't have the lights." The man looked excited.

Jibbawk turned the beetle over and watched it struggle. "It's just like the stories in my youth," he said quietly.

"All you do is sit and let it bite you. Others will come, a lot of them. Then you will become immortal."

Jibbawk wasn't listening to the old man anymore. He knew what he could become; the most powerful Shadic in the galaxy. He watched the lights flicker and change color. Such a beautiful creature.

Rain started falling from the upper canopy, landing on Jibbawk in big cold drops. He took the beetle and brought it up to his neck where the quills were the smallest and non-threatening. "If you are such a creature, give me your gift of everlasting life. I will retake thiss land and be one of your Infinite Rulerss."

The beetle's legs grabbed the skin of Jibbawk, and he let go of its shell. It bit and stayed locked onto Jibbawk's skin. The pain was great, but nothing he

couldn't handle. He sat reverently on a mossy rock, surrounded by tall, thick tree trunks.

The undergrowth started moving. A thousand beetles came out of the odd-looking bushes and from between the rough, flecked stones. The old man quickly got out of the way. The beetles crawled all over Jibbawk, biting. The swarm covered him from head to claw. The pain made Jibbawk's eyes water and his beak clench so tight he thought it would chip. Every muscle spasmed.

The old man leaned close to Jibbawk. "Sorry to trick you, you piece of garbage. See, the Lupine told me not to let them bite. If they did, they'd kill you. It's their blood I was after. It has unusual healing properties and my wife is very sick." The old man smirked. "And now that you've lowered a rope down here, I can get out." The old man laughed out loud. "I'm positive the Elders of Fifty, the ones that have been planning your overthrow for the last two years, will be thrilled when I bring them to your dead body. They'll give me all the Hubbu pollen I need so I can get home." The old man rushed off, whistling a tune.

Jibbawk tried to get up but was paralyzed. Then all went black, and the pain vanished.

He woke some time later and tried to move,

but he could not. He could see, but the light was different. It was tinted red. Jibbawk thought about moving. He imagined every muscle working in concert until he could sit. Finally, he sat up.

Next to him was the body of a Shadic. Jibbawk jumped, startled. The Shadic didn't move. It was dead. Jibbawk tried to reach out to touch the Shadic and when he did, he didn't recognize his own claws. He was a moving, churning, clumped collection of screps. At first, he thought the beetles were still covering his body, but when he slapped at the beetles with his other hand, the beetles fell apart, leaving nothing behind. There was no hand under the insect swarm, no arm, no body at all. He *was* the beetles.

Jibbawk couldn't feel himself breathe, nor hear his heart beat. His mind was still intact, his voice still strong in his thoughts. He laughed hysterically and looked at the Shadic that lay next to him, dead. It was *his* body, colorless and as still as the stones.

Jibbawk stood. The beetles easily formed legs. His new body resembled the Shadic form he was used to, but gone were his quills.

A shriek-bird landed on a sparse branch a dozen feet up and cried out. Its shrill song unnerved

Jibbawk, even more so. He visualized eating the bird alive, however, he was nothing now. Just an amalgamation of powerless and useless beetles. Jibbawk was as good as dead.

The bird's incessant shrieking drew out the rage in Jibbawk, causing a group of beetles to break away and skitter up the tree trunk. They moved silently and stealthily and filled the underside of the branch below the bird. One of the smaller beetles climbed out of the mass and showed itself. The bird saw the beetle and hoped so that it could snack on the insect. When the bird tried, a dozen other beetles, unsheathed their wings and quickly swarmed the startled bird, moving with shocking speed. They bit with powerful mandibles, throwing bits of red and yellow feathers into the air. The bird flapped its wings, but fell.

It landed at Jibbawk's feet, twitching. Jibbawk unleashed a thousand more beetles and within moments, the entire carcass was devoured, leaving only the bones. A hunger came over Jibbawk, like an electric vibration. He needed more.

The insects had a powerful bite, that much he could attest too, and a toxin that killed his physical form and the bird, but he wondered if he could do any real damage to a Lan Darrian or to Ricky Boldary as they would undoubtedly fight back. Well, there's only one way to find out.

His beetle-legs carried him to the edge of the sinkhole. Jibbawk ordered them to climb. They broke apart and scampered up the rock as easily as any beetle could. Some flew, but they had a very short range.

Jibbawk's mind seem to rest in the largest screb, the leader of them. It was the one he caught, the one with all the lights in its shell.

Jibbawk's beetles climbed to the top of the sinkhole the reformed his Shadic-like body. He stood and watched as the sun turned the horizon a blood red, looking toward Dantia. Next to him was a tall purple pyramid flower, the most popular on Lan Darr. A few beetles flew to the plants stalk and with only a couple powerful bites, beheaded the flower, sending it to the grass to rot.

Jibbawk vowed to hunt down the old man that tricked him and devour his body, one bite at a time. Then afterward, he would figure out how to use his new body to terrorize the people of Dantia. They would regret removing him from power. They would have no choice but to let him back on his throne

so that he may be the first of the Immortal Rulers. Only then will he avenge his father and remove Cal-kaw from his seat on Cicanth. No, his plans were not spoiled. Jibbawk would still become the most powerful Shadic the stars had ever seen.

The End is Only the Beginning

You've just read Book 3 of the Heroes of Distant Planets Series. I want you to know that I appreciate your time and energy and hope you enjoyed my story. Now, don't go away so fast. This book is the prequel to the series. I know you'll love the first two books and hopefully, I'll win you over as a lifetime fan. Read more tales about Lan Darr, Jibbawk and the adventures of an unlikely hero named Allan Westerfield and Ricky Boldary in Book 1 and 2 of the Heroes of Distant Planets Series:

Strange Lands

A teen, Allan Westerfield, finds himself running from Jibbawk on a planet he does not recognize. How did he get there? How will he get home? How can he, a paraplegic, move through Lan Darr without his wheelchair. **Read book 1 today!** http://AndersonAtlas.com/StrangeLands

Return to Lan Darr

Jibbawk escapes exile, only to hunt Allan and Asantia. The second book of the Heroes of Distant Planet Series cranks up the excitement, the mystery and even the humor. http://AndersonAtlas.com/ReturnToLanDarr

Discover more Books by Anderson Atlas!
AndersonAtlas.com

About the Author

Anderson Atlas is an author and illustrator that lives in the hot Sonoran Desert among scaled survivors, steely eye hawks and majestic saguaros. He's an avid observer, reader and story teller.

Please, if you like his stories, help him out and leave a review on Amazon or Goodreads or simply stay in touch by signing up for his readers group at AndersonAtlas.com

Anderson Atlas

Copyright 2015 Anderson Atlas
andersonatlas.com
Published by Synesthesia Books
synesthesiabooks.com

Immortal Shadow